Body and Soul

Edited by DAVID MARCUS

poolbeg press

Ireland is a country in which, almost by edict, procreation has been actively encouraged while sex has been actively discouraged. While this paradox has tended to drive sex underground, so to speak, and has given birth to certain misconceptions about the sexual nature of the Irish, in the country's literature sex has obstinately refused to lower its head, ugly or otherwise.

These twelve stories by various hands, many of whom are among the world's greatest short story writers, depict — frankly and sympathetically — different aspects of sex and the Irish.

Contents

First published 1979 by Poolbeg Press Ltd.,
Knocksedan House, Swords,
Co. Dublin, Ireland.

The generous assistance of An Comhairle Ealaion
(The Arts Council) in the publication of this book
is gratefully acknowledged.

Designed by Steven Hope
Cover by Robert Ballagh

Printed by Cahill Printers Limited,
East Wall Road, Dublin 3.

Acknowledgements

To the author and Weidenfeld and Nicolson Ltd., for "Ways" from *Mrs Reinhardt and other stories* by Edna O'Brien.
To the author and Faber and Faber Ltd., for "Sierra Leone" from *Getting Through* by John McGahern.
To the author and Faber and Faber Ltd., for "An Aspect of the Rising" from *Dance the Dance* by Tom Mac Intyre.
To the author and The Bodley Head Ltd., for "An Evening with John Joe Dempsey" from *The Ballroom of Romance and other stories* by William Trevor.
To the author and Constable & Co., Ltd., for "The Talking Trees" from *Selected Stories* by Sean O'Faolain.
To the editors of the following: *Threshold* for "Beginnings" by John Morrow; *The Kilkenny Magazine* for "Priest and People" by Kevin Casey; *Transatlantic Review* for "The Compromise" by Tim Pat Coogan; *The Irish Press* for "Trio" by Helen Lucy Burke and "Humanae Vitae" (previously entitled "Eine Kleine Nachtmusik") by Val Mulkerns which first appeared in the "New Irish Writing" page.
"News for the Church" by Frank O'Connor is reprinted with the kind permission of A. D. Peters and Co., Ltd.
"A Sexual Relationship" by Gillman Noonan was first published by Poolbeg Press Ltd., in his collection of that name.

SEAN O'FAOLAIN

The Talking Trees

There were four of them in the same class at the Red Abbey, all under fifteen. They met every night in Mrs. Coffey's sweetshop at the top of the Victoria Road to play the fruit machine, smoke fags and talk about girls. Not that they really talked about them — they just winked, leered, nudged one another, laughed, grunted and groaned about them, or said things like 'See her legs?' 'Yaroosh!' 'Wham!' 'Ouch!' 'Ooof!' or 'If only, if only!' But if anybody said, 'Only what?' they would not have known precisely what. They knew nothing precisely about girls, they wanted to know everything precisely about girls, there was nobody to tell them all the things they wanted to know about girls and what they thought they wanted to do with them. Aching and wanting, not knowing, half guessing, they dreamed of clouds upon clouds of fat, pink, soft, ardent girls billowing towards them across the horizon of their future. They might just as well have been dreaming of pink porpoises moaning at their feet for love.

In the sweetshop the tall glass jars of coloured sweets shone in the bright lights. The one-armed fruit-machine went zing. Now and again girls from Saint Monica's came in to buy sweets, giggle roguishly and over-pointedly ignore them. Mrs. Coffey was young, buxom, fairhaired, blue-eyed and very good-looking. They admired her so much that one night when Georgie Watchman whispered to them that she had fine bubs Dick Franks told him curtly not to be so coarse, and Jimmy Sullivan said in his most toploftical voice, 'Georgie Watchman, you should be jolly well ashamed of yourself, you are no gentleman,' and

Tommy Gong Gong said nothing but nodded his head as insistently as a ventriloquist's dummy.

Tommy's real name was Tommy Flynn, but he was younger than any of them so that neither he nor they were ever quite sure that he ought to belong to the gang at all. To show it they called him all sorts of nicknames, like Inch because he was so small; Fatty because he was so puppy-fat; Pigeon because he had a chest like a woman; Gong Gong because after long bouts of silence he had a way of suddenly spraying them with wild bursts of talk like a fire alarm attached to a garden sprinkler.

That night all Georgie Watchman did was to make a rude blubberlip noise at Dick Franks. But he never again said anything about Mrs. Coffey. They looked up to Dick. He was the oldest of them. He had long eyelashes like a girl, perfect manners, the sweetest smile and the softest voice. He had been to two English boarding schools, Ampleforth and Downside, and in Ireland to three, Clongowes, Castleknock and Rockwell, and been expelled from all five of them. After that his mother had made his father retire from the Indian Civil, come back to the old family house in Cork and, as a last hope, send her darling Dicky to the Red Abbey day-school. He smoked a corncob pipe and dressed in droopy plus fours with cheqered stockings and red flares, as if he was always jut coming from or going to the golf course. He played cricket and tennis, games that no other boy at the Red Abbey could afford to play. They saw him as the typical school-captain they read about in English boys' papers like *The Gem* and *The Magnet, The Boys' Own Paper, The Captain* and *Chums,* which was where they got all those swanky words like Wham, Ouch, Yaroosh, Ooof and Jolly Well. He was their Tom Brown, their Bob Cherry, their Tom Merry, those heroes who were always leading Greyfriars School or Blackfriars School to victory on the cricket field amid the cap-tossing huzzas of the juniors and the admiring smiles of visiting parents. It never occurred to them that *The Magnet* or *The Gem* would have seen all four of them as perfect models for some such story as *The Cads of Greyfriars,* or *The Bounders of Blackfriars,* low types given to secret smoking in the spinneys, drinking in The Dead Woman's Inn, or cheating at examinations, or, worst crime of all, betting on horses with redfaced bookies' touts down from London, while the rest of the school was practising at the nets — a quartet of rotters fated to be caned ceremoniously in the last chapter before the entire awestruck school, and then whistled off at dead of night back to their heartbroken fathers and mothers.

It could not have occurred to them because these crimes did not exist at the Red Abbey. Smoking? At the Red Abbey any boy who wanted to was free to smoke himself into a galloping consumption so long as he did it off the premises, in the jakes or up the chimney. Betting? Brother Julius was always passing fellows sixpence or even a bob to put on an uncle's or a cousin's horse at Leopardstown or the Curragh. In the memory of man no boy had ever been caned ceremoniously for anything. Fellows were just leathered all day long for not doing their homework, or playing hooky from school, or giving lip, or fighting in class — and they were leathered hard. Two years ago Jimmy Sullivan had been given six swingers on each hand with the sharp edge of a metre-long ruler for pouring the contents of an inkwell over Georgie Watchman's head in the middle of a history lesson about the Trojan Wars, in spite of his wailing explanation that he had only done it because he thought Georgie Watchman was a scut and all Trojans were blacks. Drink? They did not drink only because they were too poor. While, as for what *The Magnet* and *The Gem* really meant by 'petting' — which, they dimly understood, was some sort of depravity that no decent English boy would like to see mentioned in print — hardly a week passed that some brother did not say that a hard problem in algebra, or a leaky pen, or a window that would not open or shut was 'a blooming bugger'.

There was the day when little Brother Angelo gathered half a dozen boys about him at playtime to help him with a crossword puzzle.

'Do any of ye,' he asked, 'know what Notorious Conduct could be in seven letters?'

'Buggery?' Georgie suggested mock-innocently.

'Please be serious!' Angelo said. 'This is about Conduct.'

When the solution turned out to be *Jezebel,* little Angelo threw up his hands, said it must be some queer kind of foreign woman and declared that the whole thing was a blooming bugger. Or there was that other day when old Brother Expeditus started to tell them about the strict lives and simple food of Dominican priests and Trappist monks. When Georgie said, 'No tarts, Brother?' Expeditus had laughed loud and long.

'No, Georgie!' he chuckled. 'No pastries of any kind.'

They might as well have been in school in Arcadia. And every other school about them seemed to be just as hopeless. In fact they might have gone on dreaming of pink porpoises for years if it was not for a small thing that Gong Gong told them one October night in the sweetshop. He sprayed them with the news that his sister Jenny had been thrown out of class that morning in Saint Monica's for turning up with a red ribbon in her hair, a mother-of-pearl brooch at her neck and smelling of scent.

'Ould Sister Eustasia,' he fizzled, 'made her go out in the yard and wash herself under the tap, she said they didn't want any girls in their school who had notions.'

The three gazed at one another, and began at once to discuss all the possible sexy meanings of notions. Georgie had a pocket dictionary. 'An ingenious contrivance'? 'An imperfect conception (*U.S.*)'? 'Small wares'? It did not make sense. Finally they turned to Mrs. Coffey. She laughed, nodded towards two giggling girls in the shop who were eating that gummy kind of block toffee that can gag you for half an hour, and said, 'Why don't you ask *them*?' Georgie approached them most politely.

'Pardon me ladies, but do you by any chance happen to have notions?'

The two girls stared at one another with cow's eyes,

blushed scarlet and fled from the shop shrieking with laughter. Clearly a notion was very sexy.

'Georgie!' Dick pleaded. 'You're the only one who knows anything. What in heaven's name is it?'

When Georgie had to confess himself stumped they knew at last that their situation was desperate. Up to now Georgie had always been able to produce some sort of answer, right or wrong, to all their questions. He was the one who, to their disgust, told them what he called conraception meant. He was the one who had explained to them that all babies are delivered from the navel of the mother. He was the one who had warned them that if a fellow kissed a bad woman he would get covered by leprosy from head to foot. The son of a Head Constable, living in the police barracks, he had collected his facts simply by listening as quietly as a mouse to the other four policemen lolling in the dayroom of the barracks with their collars open, reading the sporting pages of *The Freeman's Journal,* slowly creasing their polls and talking about colts, fillies, cows, calves, bulls and bullocks and 'the mysteerious nachure of all faymale wimmen'. He had also gathered a lot of useful stuff by dutiful attendance since the age of eleven at the meetings and marchings of the Protestant Boys' Brigade, and from a devoted study of the Bible. And here he was, stumped by a nun!

Dick lifted his beautiful eyelashes at the three of them, jerked his head and led them out on the pavement.

'I have a plan,' he said quietly. 'I've been thinking of it for some time. Chaps! Why don't we see everything with our own eyes?' And he threw them into excited discussion by mentioning a name. 'Daisy Bolster?'

Always near every school, there is a Daisy Bolster — the fast girl whom everybody has heard about and nobody knows. They had all seen her at a distance. Tall, a bit skinny, long legs, dark eyes, lids heavy as the dimmers of a car lamp, prominent white teeth, and her lower lip always gleaming wet. She could be as old as seventeen. Maybe even eighteen. She wore her hair up. Dick told them that he had met her once at the tennis club with four or five other fellows around her and that she had laughed and winked very boldly all the time. Georgie said that he once heard a fellow in school say, 'She goes with boys.' Gong Gong bubbled that that was true because his sister Jenny told him that a girl named Daisy Bolster had been thrown out of school three years ago for talking to a boy outside the convent gate. At this Georgie flew into a terrible rage.

'You stupid slob!' he roared. 'Don't you know yet that when anybody says a boy and a girl are talking to one another it means they're doing you-know-what?'

'I don't know you-know-what,' Gong Gong wailed. 'What what?'

'I heard a fellow say,' Jimmy Sullivan revealed solemnly, 'that she has no father and that her mother is no better than she should be.'

Dick said in approving tones that he had once met another fellow who had heard her telling some very daring stories.

'Do you think she would show us for a quid?'

Before they parted on the pavement that night they were talking not about a girl but about a fable. Once a girl like that gets her name up she always ends up as a myth, and for a generation afterwards, maybe more, it is the myth that persists. 'Do you remember,' some old chap will wheeze, 'that girl Daisy Bolster? She used to live up the Mardyke. We used to say she was fast.' The other old boy will nod knowingly, the two of them will look at one another inquisitively, neither will admit anything, remembering only the long, dark avenue, its dim gas-lamps, the stars hooked in its trees.

Within a month Dick had fixed it. Their only trouble after that was to collect the money and to decide whether Gong Gong should be allowed to come with them.

Dick fixed that, too, at a final special meeting in the sweet-shop. Taking his pipe from between his lips, he looked speculatively at Gong Gong, who looked up at him with eyes big as plums, trembling between the terror of being told he could not come with them and the greater terror of being told that he could.

'Tell me, Gong Gong,' Dick said politely, 'what exactly does your father do?'

'He's a tailor,' Tommy said, blushing a bit at having to confess it, knowing that Jimmy's dad was a bank clerk, that Georgie's was a Head Constable, and that Dick's had been a Commissioner in the Punjab.

'Very fine profession,' Dick said kindly. 'Gentleman's Tailor and Outfitter. I see. Flynn and Company? Or is it Flynn and Sons? Have I seen his emporium?'

'Ah, no!' Tommy said, by now as red as a radish. 'He's not that sort of a tailor at all, he doesn't build suits, ye know, that's a different trade altogether, he works with me mother at home in Tuckey Street, he tucks things in and he lets things out, he's what they call a mender and turner, me brother Turlough had this suit I have on me now before I got it, you can see he's very good at his job, he's a real dab . . .'

Dick let him run on, nodding sympathetically — meaning to convey to the others that they really could not expect a fellow to know much about girls if his father spent his life mending and turning old clothes in some side alley called Tuckey Street.

'Do you fully realise, Gong Gong, that we are proposing to behold the ultimate female beauty?'

'You mean,' Gong Gong smiled fearfully, 'that she'll only be wearing her nightie?'

Georgie Watchman turned from him in disgust to the fruit-machine. Dick smiled on.

'The thought had not occurred to me,' he said. 'I wonder, Gong Gong, where do you get all those absolutely filthy ideas. If we subscribe seventeen and sixpence, do you think you can contribute half-a-crown?'

'I could feck it, I suppose.'

Dick raised his eyelashes.

'Feck?'

Gong Gong looked shamedly at the tiles.
'I mean steal,' he whispered.
'Don't they give you any pocket money?'
'They give me threepence a week.'
'Well, we have only a week to go. If you can, what was your word, feck half-a-crown, you may come.'
The night chosen was a Saturday — her mother always went to town on Saturdays; the time of meeting, five o'clock exactly; the place, the entrance to the Mardyke Walk.
On any other occasion it would have been a gloomy spot for a rendezvous. For adventure, perfect. A long tree-lined avenue, with, on one side, a few scattered houses and high enclosing walls; on the other side the small canal whose deep dyke had given it its name. Secluded, no traffic allowed inside the gates, complete silence. A place where men came every night to stand with their girls behind the elm trees kissing and whispering for hours. Dick and Georgie were there on the dot of five. Then Jimmy Sullivan came swiftly loping. From where they stood, under a tree just beyond the porter's lodge, trembling with anticipation, they could see clearly for only about a hundred yards up the long tunnel of elms lit by the first stars above the boughs, one tawny window streaming across a dank garden, and beyond that a feeble perspective of pendant lamps fading dimly away into the blue November dusk. Within another half-hour the avenue would be pitch black between those meagre pools of light.
Her instructions had been precise. In separate pairs, at exactly half-past five, away up there beyond the last lamp, where they would be invisible as cockroaches, they must gather outside her house.
'You won't be able even to see one another,' she had said gleefully to Dick, who had stared coldly at her, wondering how often she had stood behind a tree with some fellow who would not have been able to see her face.
Every light in the house would be out except for the fanlight over the door.

'Ooo!' she had giggled. 'It will be terribly oohey. You won't hear a sound but the branches squeaking. You must come along to my door. You must leave the other fellows to watch from behind the trees. You must give two short rings. Once, twice. And then give a long ring, and wait.' She had started to whisper the rest, her hands by her sides clawing her dress in her excitement. 'The fanlight will go out if my mother isn't at home. The door will open slowly. You must step into the dark hall. A hand will take your hand. You won't know whose hand it is. It will be like something out of Sherlock Holmes. You will be simply terrified. You won't know what I'm wearing. For all you'll know I might be wearing nothing at all!'

He must leave the door ajar. The others must follow him one by one. After that . . .

It was eleven minutes past five and Gong Gong had not yet come. Already three women had passed up the Mardyke carrying parcels, hurrying home to their warm fires, forerunners of the home-for-tea crowd. When they had passed out of sight Georgie growled, 'When that slob comes I'm going to put my boot up his backside.' Dick, calmly puffing his corncob, gazing wearily up at the stars, laughed tolerantly and said, 'Now Georgie, don't be impatient. We shall see all! We shall at last know all!'

Georgie sighed and decided to be weary too.

'I hope,' he drawled, 'this poor frail isn't going to let us down!'

For three more minutes they waited in silence and then Jimmy Sullivan let out a cry of relief. There was the small figure hastening towards them along the Dyke Parade from one lamppost to another.

'Puffing and panting as usual, I suppose,' Dick chuckled. 'And exactly fourteen minutes late.'

'I hope to God,' Jimmy said, 'he has our pound note. I don't know in hell why you made that slob our treasurer.'

'Because he is poor,' Dick said quietly. 'We would have spent it.'

He came panting up to them, planted a black violin case

against the tree and began rummaging in his pockets for the money.

'I'm supposed to be at a music lesson, that's me alibi, me father always wanted to be a musician but he got married instead, he plays the cello, me brother Turlough plays the clarinet, me sister Jenny plays the viola, we have quartets, I sold a Haydn quartet for one and six, I had to borrow sixpence from Jenny, and I fecked the last sixpence from me mother's purse, that's what kept me so late . . .'

They were not listening, staring into the soiled and puckered handkerchief he was unravelling to point out, one by one, a crumpled half-note, two half-crowns, two shillings and a sixpenny bit.

'That's all yeers, and here's mine. Six threepenny bits for the quartet. That's one and six. Here's Jenny's five pennies and two ha'pence. That makes two bob. And here's the tanner I just fecked from me mother's purse. That makes my two and sixpence.'

Eagerly he poured the mess into Dick's hands. At the sight of the jumble Dick roared at him.

'I told you, you bloody little fool, to bring a pound note!'

'You told me to bring a pound.'

'I said a pound note. I can't give this dog's breakfast to a girl like Daisy Bolster.'

'You said a pound.'

They all began to squabble. Jimmy Sullivan shoved Gong Gong. Georgie punched him. Dick shoved Georgie. Jimmy defended Georgie with 'We should never have let that slob come with us.' Gong Gong shouted, 'Who's a slob?' and swiped at him. Jimmy shoved him again so that he fell over his violin case, and a man passing home to his tea shouted at them, 'Stop beating that little boy at once!'

Tactfully they cowered. Dick helped Gong Gong to his feet. Georgie dusted him lovingly. Jimmy retrieved his cap, put it back crookedly on his head and patted him kindly. Dick explained in his best Ampleforth accent that they had merely been having 'a trifling discussion', and 'our young friend here tripped over his suitcase'. The man surveyed them dubiously, growled something and went on his way. When he was gone Georgie pulled out his pocketbook, handed a brand-new pound note to Dick and grabbed the dirty jumble of cash. Dick at once said, 'Quick march! Two by two!' and strode off ahead of the others, side by side with Tommy in his crooked cap, lugging his dusty violin case, into the deepening dark.

They passed nobody. They heard nothing. They saw only the few lights in the sparse houses along the left of the Mardyke. On the other side was the silent, railed-in stream. When they came in silence to the wide expanse of the cricket field the sky dropped a blazing veil of stars behind the outfield nets. When they passed the gates of the railed-in public park, locked for the night, darkness returned between the walls to their left and the overgrown laurels glistening behind the tall railings on their right. Here Tommy stopped dead, hooped fearfully towards the laurels.

'What's up with you?' Dick snapped at him.

'I hear a noise, me father told me once how a man murdered a woman in there for her gold watch, he said men do terrible things like that because of bad women, he said that that man was hanged by the neck in Cork Jail, he said that was the last time the black flag flew on top of the jail. Dick! I don't want to go on!'

Dick peered at the phosphorescent dial of his watch, and strode ahead, staring at the next feeble lamp hanging crookedly from its black iron arch. Tommy had to trot to catch up with him.

'We know,' Dick said, 'that she has long legs. Her breasts will be white and small.'

'I won't look!' Tommy moaned.

'Then don't look!'

Panting, otherwise silently, they hurried past the old corrugated iron building that had once been a roller-skating rink and was now empty and abandoned. After the last lamp the night became impenetrable, then her house rose slowly to their left against the starlight. It was square, tall, solid, brick-fronted, three-storied and jet-black against the stars except for its half-moon fanlight. They walked a few yards past it and halted, panting, behind a tree. The only sound was the squeaking of a branch over their heads. Looking backwards, they saw Georgie and Jimmy approaching under the last lamp. Looking forwards, they saw a brightly lit tram, on its way outward from the city, pass the far end of the tunnel, briefly light its maw and black it out again. Beyond that lay wide fields and the silent river. Dick said, 'Tell them to follow me if the fanlight goes out,' and disappeared.

Alone under the tree, backed still by the park, Tommy looked across to the far heights of Sunday's Well dotted with the lights of a thousand suburban houses. He clasped his fiddle case before him like a shield. He had to force himself not to run away towards where another bright tram would rattle him back to the city. Suddenly he saw the fanlight go out. Strings in the air throbbed and faded. Was somebody playing a cello? His father bowed over his cello, jacket off, shirt-sleeves rolled up, entered the Haydn; beside him Jenny waited, chin sideways over the viola, bosom lifted, bow poised, the tendons of her frail wrist hollowed by the lamplight, Turlough facing them lipped a thinner reed. His mother sat shawled by the fire, tapping the beat with her toe. Georgie and Jimmy joined him.

'Where's Dick?' Georgie whispered urgently.

'Did I hear music?' he gasped.

Georgie vanished, and again the strings came and faded. Jimmy whispered. 'Has she a gramophone?' Then they could hear nothing but the faint rattle of the vanished tram. When Jimmy slid away from him, he raced madly up into the darkness, and then stopped halfway to the tunnel's end. He did not have the penny to pay for the tram. He turned and raced as madly back the way he had come, down past her house, down to where the gleam of the laurels hid the murdered woman, and stopped again. He heart a rustling noise. A rat? He looked back, thought of her long legs and her small, white breasts, and found himself walking heavily back to her garden gate, his heart pounding. He entered the path, fumbled for the dark door, pressed against it, felt it slew open under his hand, stepped cautiously into the dark hallway, closed the door, saw nothing, heard nothing, stepped onward and fell clattering on the tiles over his violin case.

A door opened. He saw firelight flicker on shining shin-bones and bare knees. Fearfully, his eyes moved upwards. She was wearing nothing but gym knickers. He saw two small birds, white, soft, rosy-tipped. Transfixed by joy he stared and stared at them. Her black hair hung over her narrow shoulders. She laughed down at him with white teeth and wordlessly gestured him to get up and come in. He faltered after her white back and stood inside the door. The only light was from the fire.

Nobody heeded him. Dick stood by the corner of the mantelpiece, one palm flat on it, his other hand holding his trembling corncob. He was peering coldly at her. His eyelashes almost met. Georgie lay sprawled in a chintzy armchair on the other side of the fire wearily flicking the ash from a black cigarette into the fender. Opposite him Jimmy Sullivan sat on the edge of a chair, his elbows on his knees, his eyeballs sticking out as if he had just swallowed something hot, hard and raw. Nobody said a word.

She stood in the centre of the carpet, looking guardedly from one to the other of them out of her hooded eyes, her thumbs inside the elastic of her gym knickers. Slowly she began to press her knickers down over her hips. When Georgie suddenly whispered 'The seventh veil!' he at once wanted to batter him over the head with his fiddle case, to shout at her to stop, to shout at them that they had seen everything, to shout that they must look no more. Instead, he lowered his head so that he saw nothing but her bare toes. Her last covering slid to the carpet. He heard three long gasps, became aware that Dick's pipe had fallen to the floor, that Georgie had started straight up, one fist lifted as if he was going to strike her, and that Jimmy had covered his face with his two hands.

A coal tinkled from the fire to the fender. With averted eyes he went to it, knelt before it, wet his fingers with his spittle as he had often seen his mother do, deftly laid the coal back on the fire and remained so far a moment watching it light up again. Then he sidled back to his violin case, walked out into the hall, flung open the door on the sky of stars and straightway started to race the whole length of the Mardyke from pool to pool of light in three gasping spurts.

After the first spurt he stood gasping until his heart had stopped hammering. He heard a girl laughing softly behind a tree. Just before his second halt he saw ahead of him a man and a woman approaching him arm in arm, but when he came up to where they should have been they too had become invisible. Halted, breathing, listening, he heard their murmuring somewhere in the dark. At his third panting rest he heard an invisible girl say, 'Oh, no, oh no!' and a man's urgent voice say, 'But yes, but yes!' He felt that behind every tree there were kissing lovers, and without stopping he ran the gauntlet between them until he had emerged from the Mardyke among the bright lights of the city. Then, at last, the sweat cooling on his forehead, he was standing outside the shuttered plumber's shop above which they lived. Slowly he climbed the bare stairs to their floor and their door. He paused for a moment to look up through the windows at the stars, opened the door and went in.

Four heads around the supper table turned to look up inquiringly at him. At one end of the table his mother sat wearing her blue apron. At the other end his father sat, in his rolled-up shirt-sleeves as if he had only just laid down the pressing iron. Turlough gulped his food. Jenny was smiling mockingly at him. She had the red ribbon in her hair and the mother-of-pearl brooch at her neck.

'You're bloody late,' his father said crossly. 'What the hell kept you? I hope you came straight home from your lesson. What way did you come? Did you meet anybody or talk to anybody? You know I don't want any loitering at night. I hope you weren't cadeying with any blackguards? Sit down, sir, and eat your supper. Or did your lordship expect us to wait for you? What did you play tonight? What did Professor Hartmann give you to practise for your next lesson?'

He sat in his place. His mother filled his plate and they all ate in silence.

Always the questions! Always talking talking at him! They never let him alone for a minute. His hands sank. She was so lovely. So white. So soft. So pink. His mother said gently, 'You're not eating, Tommy. Are you all right?'

He said, 'Yes, yes, I'm fine, Mother.'

Like birds. Like stars. Like music.

His mother said, 'You are very silent tonight, Tommy. You usually have a lot of talk after you've been to Professor Hartmann. What are you thinking of?'

'They were so beautiful!' he blurted.

'What was so bloody beautiful!' his father rasped. 'What are you blathering about?'

'The stars,' he said hastily.

Jenny laughed. His father frowned. Silence returned.

He knew that he would never again go back to the sweetshop. They would only want to talk and talk about her. They would want to bring everything out into the light, boasting and smirking about her, taunting him for having run away. He would be happy forever if only he could walk every night of his life up the dark Mardyke, hearing nothing but a girl's laugh from behind a tree, a branch squeaking and the far-off rattle of a lost tram; walk on and on, deeper and deeper into the darkness until he could see nothing but one tall house whose fanlight she would never put out again. The doorbell might ring, but she would not hear it. The door might be answered, but not by her. She would be gone. He had known it ever since he heard her laughing softly by his side as they ran away together, for ever and ever, between those talking trees.

GILLMAN NOONAN

A Sexual Relationship

If Sean Kenny were to admit the truth about why he thought he was attractive to women he would probably skip, lightly and winningly, over all the more obvious reasons—such as his tall, athletic figure, his gravity that belied his twenty-five years, or his sense of humour combined with just the right mixture of interest in external things and those of the spirit — and set most store by his carefully cultivated manner of not appearing to give a damn about them. If this was cynicism, it worked, and Sean Kenny was only interested in what worked. Quite enough things, he felt sure, would not work out later in life, but right now if they were working like this, well, why interfere? He was enjoying himself. If a girl was prepared to go along with his non-committal way and sleep with him, wasn't that her affair? And if afterwards — perhaps with her eye on the ring — she called him conceited and inaccessible, or even a fraud, she was quite entitled to do so once she didn't annoy him further. For once a girl began to dig below the skin it didn't work any more and Kenny put a speedy end to it. He had no intention of marrying for some time, so love and tantrums were definitely out.

His nonchalant approach seemed to work too in the case of Helga Liebig, his German teacher. He wasn't especially attracted to her as a person — at least to the extent that he knew her from class and intermittent conversations in the tea breaks — but her body was superb. The first evening he came to the language institute she ascended the stairs before him displaying the most exquisite legs he had ever seen. Her thighs were long and tanned with just the right amount of flesh on them, and as far as he could see the other parts attached to them were of equally fine proportions. True, he was a bit disappointed in her face when he sat down and had a chance to study her. She had a kind of lopsided Barbra Streisand face, only funnier. And it seemed too small for her body. It also had its own peculiar sense of humour. There were times when she stood with the chalk in her hand chuckling away idiotically while the class looked on wondering where the joke was. But that body made up for a lot of foolishness. Kenny saw it dimly outlined in a bedroom door, softly tense, provocatively akimbo in a whisper of lace, murmuring '*Kommst du, Liebling?*'

Needless to say, in those intermittent conversations over tea Kenny gave no hint of harbouring any such visions of sensual dalliance. She was a sophisticated woman of about twenty-seven who spoke fluent English and would obviously be unimpressed by any amateurish posturing. So while other male members of the class made animated conversation with Helga Liebig and playfully shouted invitations to each other to have *noch eine Tasse Tee* or *noch einen Kuchen* (it is *einen,* is it, Fräulein Liebig?), Kenny stood slightly apart, of the group yet not of it, and quietly sipped his tea. He was not a snob, certainly not a pipe and cravat type, but he liked reserve, and found that women liked men who had reserve. Sometimes he felt Helga regarding him and then, as though he had just happened to look at her, he ventured a throwaway boyish grin that tactfully fell short of a wink. And if he did approach her with a question, he made sure it reflected the higher echelons of management into which he was steadily climbing.

It was working, but when after a couple of months it came to actually asking her out she beat him — to his immense satisfaction — by a head. She had these two tickets to a recital of German music. Would he like to come? Love to. Great. Where did she live? Herbert Road? Better still. On his way from Blackrock. Pick her up what time?

Great. See you then, Helga.

He was very pleased with himself. Perhaps there would be problems, perhaps she had set her mind on marrying a cultured (yes he was, well read and quite nifty on the fiddle) young Irishman with a future, perhaps deep down she was full of German fundamentalism, perhaps she was even a virgin (he doubted it very much) — but whatever she was he would play the game long enough for them to have a pleasant time together. He would enjoy himself, she would enjoy herself. Wasn't that what it was really all about? Then, when the relationship looked like settling into too definite a mould, basta. Even if it meant giving up classes to avoid further embarrassment. He doubted in any case if he would have the fortitude to get much beyond 'May I borrow your ball point pen, my own is kaputt.'

Her manner on their first night out was the blend of idiosyncratic vagueness and intense analysis that characterised her teaching methods. In the little place where they had a meal after the recital her mood shifted rapidly from that strange raptness in which she did a lot of tongue-clicking to herself to acute observation when she would fix her attention on a part of his face other than his eyes and hold forth on contentious issues. Kenny was not happy with any of her moods — she was not an *easy* person to talk to and he was sure now that as a person she didn't really appeal to him — but at least, within a couple of hours, she had reassuringly disposed of the more obvious hurdles in the way of spirited bed play. Many of them were swept aside in such a headlong rush that he had difficulty in keeping up with her. Was he religious? Certainly not. These mediaeval superstitions. Neither was she. She hated people who talked about God. Such a vague individual. She considered herself a feminist but of the good sort. Did he approve of . . .? He did? He approved of liberated women? He certainly did. They didn't put him off with their occasional intellectualising and so? They certainly didn't. She didn't think that marriage worked. Did he? Possibly. But he wasn't going to put it to the test for several years (that was *that* anyway!). Basically, she didn't approve at all of the nuclear family. Of the what? The nuclear family. You know, the . . . Oh, yes. No, no. He was all for nuclear disarmament. Ha, ha. You didn't have divorce in Ireland, did you? No. Her parents were divorced. Really? So were one sister and a brother. Quite a batting average, what? Yes. But of course that wasn't what really influenced her in her views on marriage. She just valued her freedom to do as she pleased. (Excellent!) And to commit herself as she pleased. Yes, that's the ticket. Live, love and be happy for tomorrow . . . Oh, no, no, she didn't quite believe in *that* philosophy. Philosophy. Pardon? I said, philosophy. What philosophy?

Phew!

Then would come another lengthy period of vague looking into the distance while he (she didn't seem to care whether he spoke or not) rummaged around for things to say, twiddling his wine glass. It was as if whatever sun of intellect shone in her occasionally took a dive into impenetrable German mists out of which it had to struggle to emerge. A few times he caught himself drifting off with her, becoming transfixed to some ethereal point on the ceiling beyond the realm of the familiar. It worried him not a little because if her sexual nature revealed similar periods of on-off activity he would have to be quick off the mark to beam in on the current while it flowed, as during a strike of the Electricity Supply Board. A two hours on, two hours off affair in which there would be a lot of dark fumblings and mutterings. Vaguely he wondered if there was a manic-depressive strain in the family.

Twice more they went out, and though the pattern of communication remained the same with Kenny allowing himself to be picked up like a leaf and spun around in little whirlpools of conversation only to be deposited then, suddenly and flatly, in some obscure corner of his experience, at least their physical intimacy increased to his satisfaction. On their second night out they danced and she pressed her long firm body to his with an unmistakable promise of greater things to come. Indeed, on the way home he thought the time was ripe when, having recovered from one of her spells of near cataleptic indifference, she again radiated willingness. But: reserve, reserve. Kenny was not a messer. Also, she had invited him to spend a quiet evening at her place on the morrow, a Saturday. Fit and relaxed with the whole evening in front of them: what better time for dalliance!

The next evening he complimented himself on his good sense when, tapping gently on the flat door, he found it on the snib and entered to hear water sloshing in the bath and a voice, redolent, it seemed, of essence of pine and rosewood, say: 'I am there in a minute, Sean. Please serve yourself to a drink.' Through the slightly open door he caught a glimpse of naked shoulders. Yes, this was it. With a touch of class. In fact, it was straight out of one of his favourite sexual fantasies. He stood for a moment in the middle of the floor indulging it. The flat was comfortable, luxurious almost with a lot of pillows and poufs and sheepskins lying about. Gentle baroque music came from the speakers on each side of the deep coal fire. Great. He helped himself to a liberal gin from a row of bottles on the sideboard.

'Any tonic?' he sang.

'Yes, in the fridge.'

Indeed, Irish girls had a lot to learn. No half-empty bottles of red biddy hidden in the loo after boozy parties. No towels and panties lying about with their hint of habitual slovenliness. Instead, the languid plash of scented water mingling with the sensuous rhythms of old music. He picked a volume of Nietzsche from the shelf and settled himself in a deep armchair. He read: 'To the despiser of the body will I speak a word. That they despise is caused by their esteem.' Great stuff.

'This Nietzsche guy is great stuff,' he called out.

'What?'

'Nietzsche. I like him.'

'Oh, ja! He has never really been understood. You

know? The freedom he wanted.'

'The physical freedom.'

'Ja! That is also a good translation.'

'Excellent,' he agreed. Kenny, the great judge of Nietzsche translations.

Quietly he read aloud, enjoying his deep rich voice: 'With the creators, the reapers, and the rejoicers will I associate.' Marvellous stuff! 'For higher ones I wait, spake Zarathustra. Stronger ones, triumphanter ones, merrier ones, for such as are built squarely in body and spirit; laughing lions must come.' *Laughing lions must come!*

Kenny leant back and yielded to a fantasy of tawny strength prowling through the forests of her nerves and sinews, a smooth vibrant force waiting for release into exultant passion. And she would give him release, this tall creature now emerging, trailing aromas of the fresh pine grove, her long gown clinging to her firm scented flesh. 'Laughing lions must come,' he said to her by way of greeting. She smiled. The power was *on*! What a body! Only a genuine, lean-hipped, ho-ho-ho bacchanalian (Falstaffian!) lion could satisfy it, carry it along in an easy lope of passion over the mysterious mental obstacles in its path. He had held that body and knew its response. Her waffle he would ignore and be a laughing lion! As she bent down groping for cigarettes under the chair a perfectly moulded breast opened to his view with its jutty rutty pinky nipple. His passion stirred and he shifted in his chair. Down, Fido. Wait for the word. She still groped, talking away. What a body! Beautiful nipple. Hi, Nipple. I'm Laughing Lion. I'd like to meet your sister. Sure, Laughing Lion, any time. . . .

She was looking at him, waiting.

He blushed. 'I'm sorry,' he said. 'What were you saying?'

'My tubes.'

'Oh.' *Tubes?* 'Having trouble?' he added faintly.

'I've just told you,' she said rather accusingly, looking at his left ear.

'Are they very bad?' he said, staring at her right nostril as though he expected one of them to appear and explain its condition. A little intestinal disorder shouldn't be too difficult to overcome, however. 'Have you any Rennies in the house?'

'Rennies? It's the eggs.'

'Very good for the indigestion.' *Eggs?*

'Do you have indigestion?'

'No, no. I thought maybe for you.'

'Did I say I had indigestion?'

He looked into her eyes. The mists were descending. He felt their cloying chill. *Laugh,* Kenny! Be a laughing lion!

'Well, Helga, tubes or no tubes you're a treat to look at. Grrr! Ho-ho! The first time I saw you I said to myself . . .'

'Sean, you must listen. You see, the tubes won't carry the eggs much longer. That's why.'

He looked at her closely. Yes, the power was definitely off, and this time it looked like a long strike of the inner light. Jesus, Kenny, you do pick 'em. E.S.B. sex, intestines all screwed up, and now galloping obfuscation. The best thing was to humour her. Maybe he would hit the right switch again.

'What's going to carry them then?'

'What?'

'The eggs.'

'That's just it. There's nothing.'

'Nothing at all, at all to carry your little eggs?'

'No, that's why, you see, I want to have a baby before it's too late.'

He sat up. *A baby?* Suddenly he began to see the light, but a different light. 'What tubes . . .' he almost shouted.

'My Fallopian tubes, of course.'

'What do you mean "of course"? Do you think I know one bloody female tube from another?'

'They're the ones that carry the eggs! I've been telling you!'

'And they're breaking down?'

'One has already and the other is shaky. I can only conceive every second month.'

'And you want to have a *baby*?'

He felt the blood coming to his face and she glared at him, her nostrils flared as though she were only now getting his real spoor. The air was electric. No strike on now. Except in passion. He felt it trickling down his belly like a lump of melting ice.

'Yes, as soon as possible.'

'And that's why you want *me*?'

'Yes.'

'You mean . . . you mean, you want me as a stud?' His upper lip was beginning to twitch. Very bad sign.

'A stud?'

'A stallion.'

'I don't understand these words.'

'You mean, you want me to . . . to service you?'

At this she went off into a peculiar kind of chuckle that never rose to the surface but seemed to slop around in her endlessly like water in a bilge. Perhaps she was seeing herself as a long sleek automobile driving into a garage where Kenny in neat overalls and a peaked cap would stick a length of tube into her tank, squirt her full and then send her on her way with a hearty slap on the rear mudguard.

'No, Sean,' she said then, becoming very serious. 'I want you to make love to me. I want to have a satisfying sexual relationship with you. But I want it to result in a baby because right now I want a baby. I want to have one before I'm thirty. I just thought it only fair to tell you because some people just do not approve of having babies. They think there are enough in the world. And if you saw me going around in a few months with a big belly you might feel responsible and everything. I don't want that.'

He sat and gaped at her. But he hardly saw her. All he saw was a thick mane of blond hair and somewhere in the middle were the small eyes of a calculating lioness. Oh, sweet Christ, Kenny. All this time you were gently stalking through the undergrowth you were being stalked yourself. The monkeys in the trees were jabbering with delight. Snakes were wrapping themselves into tiny knots with laughter. Kenny, the laughing lion. Look at him sniffing the air, dropping his sexual cruds, giving the odd low magnificent growl. Only to fade now with humiliating abruptness like that ridiculous animal on the screen. Kenny, the *instant* laughing lion.

'Let's get this straight,' he said, tossing off his gin and trying to control the twitch in his lip. 'You want to have a sexual relationship with me but only if I consent to try and make it result in a baby. Is that it?'

'Yes.'

'Otherwise, no?'

'What do you mean?'

'No baby, no fuckie?'

'Well, I have little time to waste. (Did she have a stop-watch?) Maybe in a few months it will be too late. And it is important to have sexual rapport because it may be difficult for me to conceive. (If he wasn't a good co-driver, like, she'd have to reconsider his contract). So we should start having sex as soon as possible.' (On your marks!)

One flap of her gown had slipped down revealing the long curve of her thigh. She was leaning forward intently and he could see all of her breasts. But for all she did for Kenny at that moment she might as well have been the one-buttocked old woman in Voltaire's story.

'You do realise,' he said gravely, rising from the chair (he had to take his eyes off those two lumps of flesh), the responsibility of bringing a child into the world that has no father?'

'Oh, you mustn't worry about that,' she said. 'I may marry sometime, and anyway in Germany we think differently about unmarried mothers, particularly those who *want* their babies. Also, I shall be reasonably well off soon. So I have no real problems.'

'But the point I'm making is . . .' He fingered the air in distaste as though it were suddenly soiled and sticky. 'The point I want to make is that if I refuse to become a father you will just say, all right, Sean, good-bye. I must find another man.'

'I hope you won't refuse,' she said. 'I like you. You like to appear dignified but underneath I think you are a nice sensitive boy. You also have a fine body.'

Good God! How the bitch had vetted him!

'And what a nice family I come from! Was that why you were asking me all about the artistic vein in my family and so on?'

'Well, naturally I wanted to know as much about you as possible. I mean, be fair. I could hardly have gone up to you in the tea room and said to you: Sean, I want to sleep with you because I want to make a baby. But you cannot say that I asked you any questions about your health or the health of your family. I mean there is a limit. There I must take it as if we are lovers.'

'*Love*? You just want to use me!'

'And you?' she said, sharply now, her colour suddenly rising. 'What were you thinking of before I came out of the bathroom? You were thinking of having sex with me, were you not?'

'Yes, but for the sheer enjoyment of sex, with no object in mind.'

'No object but your own pleasure.'

'And yours.'

'We can still have that. I would like a gentle tender relationship with you. It's just that I want you to know that if I conceive a baby I will have it.'

'Yes, but you planned . . .'

'Of course! Did you not plan? Did you not start planning to strip me naked and put me into bed the first time you saw me? I know when a man is looking like that.'

'You've experience, I'm sure.'

'As you have, I'm sure.'

'But what it boils down to is that you want me to come around every so often, especially in the right month, and bang you in the hope of giving you a baby.'

'Is that any different from you coming around now and then and banging me because *you* feel the need for sex?'

'It's not the same.'

'Why not?'

'Because . . . because it's not . . . functional. It's spontaneous.'

'Yes, while it lasts. Then you say good-bye, Helga. Maybe you never ring me again. I think of my pleasure too of course but in this case I'm using it for an end. That is all. And I'm trying to be honest. After all, we decided already that we did not want to fall in love or anything like that.' She added, rather smugly he thought: 'I remember you being almost adamant about that.'

'You're a shrewd one, aren't you?'

'No shrewder than you seem to be.'

A polar air had entered their exchange. She had gathered her gown tightly about her, folding her arms across her stomach as though the baby were already in there and she were determined to defend it. He was disliking her intensely.

'Why don't you go back to your own country where it might be easier to find a good stud?' He failed to keep the sneer out of his voice.

'Why should it be difficult here? I mean, men are men.'

'Go on!'

'And I like Irishmen. Some of them. Some of them are rather *too* masculine for my taste.' She was very angry now. Her tongue was clicking away like mad. Kenny walked about, flapping his arms. He had no roar left but he felt like roaring.

'I chose you because I liked you,' he said, suddenly leaning over her. 'I liked *you*, you understand? I desired *you*. I didn't desire a bloody womb.'

'Do you think I thought of a bloody sperm count when I looked at *you*? No, if I hadn't liked *you* (she was giving the word the same contemptuous curl) would I have chosen *you* to be the father of my child?'

'Yes, but if I refused the first fence *you* had ten other stallions champing at the bit waiting to take *my* place, hadn't you? You just wanted prick.'

'And what did you want?' She shook his hand from her shoulder. 'Eternal love?'

'You chose me at random.'

'Yes, I stuck a pin in you.'

'I knew it. Like a bloody race horse.'

'Exactly.'

They were almost nose to nose now.

'You have your race card too, haven't you?' she said. 'If one winner doesn't come up the next one will.'

'It's still not like yours.'

'No, it's more sophisticated, is it? The motives are pure, are they? Beautiful, pure, unselfish sex. But *you* must have the whip, *you* must do the riding. The purpose must be *yours.*'

'I did not want to just *service* you!' he roared.

'No, you wanted to fuck me.'

'Yes! A good old-fashioned Irish fuck with froth on it, on the basis of mutual agreement.'

'That is exactly what I wanted with you. A good sexual relationship. Passionate and tender and all the rest. Plus, if possible, a baby.'

'Oh, but with what cold, cunning, German calculation!'

'With what cold, cunning, sneaky Irish calculation were you planning to fuck me?'

They outnosed each other for a little longer. Then Kenny wheeled in fury and stalked out of the flat.

He drove straight to Blackrock, parked his car and set out to look for drinking friends. He found a few but after a while they bored him. Then he drank alone in a place where a shouting match seemed to be in progress between a mob and a television set. It just suited his mood. Until ten o'clock all he could think of was how he had been neatly roped in, broken and led to the mating paddock before he knew what was up. By half-past ten he was getting drunk and suggesting to another unsteady individual with a black coalman's face that 'by Jesus, all we need in Dublin now is a Dial a Daddy service.' He wondered if such an amenity would be subject to VAT. The coalman thought he was suggesting a Dial a Prayer service under Vatican guidance. He expressed the view that while that kind of thing would be all right for Americans and other people contemplating suicide there were enough people on the phone to God in Ireland. By eleven o'clock Kenny, drunk now, was beginning to think that there were still some aspects of the situation they hadn't discussed to his satisfaction. At closing time he was on the phone to her, but there was no reply.

At eleven o'clock the following evening Kenny was sitting in his car on Herbert Road waiting for her to appear. He had phoned her earlier in the day and she had told him that she would be out, that in fact there was little point in him calling around because she had obviously misjudged him, that he was behaving in just the kind of emotional way she had wanted to avoid, that it was better they forget all about it. He said he would still call. She said she could not stop him from doing so but she might not be alone. At which, she had hung up.

When she finally appeared it was in the company of several others including, he saw to his intense chagrin, Mick Ryan, another member of the class. He was one of these intellectual types who acted in plays and spoke six languages. 'Another Call Daddy,' Kenny said with venom into the smoke-filled interior. 'When the business world fails her she resorts to the university.' You couldn't be up to them. He would go in and screw the ass off her. If she resisted he would rape her. Then he never wanted to see her again.

There was a brief embarrassed silence after she had introduced him to the company. As a casual friend he would hardly be calling on her at that hour. Ryan threw him a smile that was like a sour swallow. Kenny showed him all his fine teeth. The hound had probably been looking forward to a pleasant nightcap with his hostess when the others had left. He probably thought he could screw in six languages too.

Conversation languished. Kenny said little, and it was apparent to all that there was some kind of tension between him and Helga. They avoided each other's eyes and conversation. A lovers' tiff, no doubt. There's nothing like a lovers' tiff to make people nervous, so about midnight there was a hushed exodus with smiles all round, leaving Kenny, strong and silent, sipping his drink beside the fire. When Helga returned she looked at him, shook her head and set about clearing things away. When everything was tidy she said, 'Well, I'm going to bed.'

'Well,' said Kenny, not to be outdone, 'I'm going to bed too.' He followed her into the bedroom. But as he went he felt that the power was definitely off again. This time in him.

She undressed quickly and hopped between the sheets. He disrobed with gravity, folding his clothes over a chair and laying out his change and key rings and things in perfect order. He glimpsed her smirk in the mirror and it maddened him.

'That fellow Ryan . . .' he began. How she had whispered with him in the hall!

'What about him?'

He leisurely slipped out of his trousers. 'He's a little runt.'

'I don't think so.'

'That fellow would take advantage of you.'

'In what way?'

'Oh, he'd want to fall for you and marry you and all that muck.'

'I'm glad I have a strong unromantic man to protect me.'

What was she smirking at? His endowment? Well, she should have thought of that before she opened the paddock gate.

With this thought he climbed in beside her, stretching down his legs and lying very still. She didn't care if he never had a name. He was an instrument. They lay still and silent for a while.

'You're a funny man,' she said then, moving closer to him.

'Why so?'

She touched his shoulders with the tips of her fingers. He was rigid.

'Well, here we are lying naked beside each other and it doesn't seem as if you're going to make love to me.'

'You're in a great hurry, aren't you?'

They looked at each other defiantly. Then, tight-lipped, she flicked down the bed clothes exposing him, and firmly held them down. Leaning on her elbow, she observed his sad lack of enthusiasm. Still resting her arm on the clothes, she squeezed the limp penis between thumb and forefinger. He started.

'Leave it,' he said between his teeth.

'Like a little sausage.'

'What did you expect him to look like? A little leg of mutton?' He was trembling. 'Don't touch him.'

'A *klitzekleine Bockwurst*.'

'Leave it, I said!' He roughly brushed her aside and snatched back the clothes. She turned away from him on her side.

'Go home, Sean.'

'Am I dismissed?'

'Oh, *lieber Gott,* go home!' She seemed close to tears. 'You only mean to humiliate me.'

'*I* humiliate *you?*' He mustered a nasty laugh. 'You paw me all over and then . . .'

'Go home, please!' She shook her head against the pillow. 'God, how I hate men!' Then, drily: 'You're probably impotent anyway.'

'Very probably. And sterile.'

'I've no doubt.'

'Out of 100 million sperm cells I probably have 395.'

'Yes, and 394 of those would be on crutches.'

It was a good line. She loved it. She loved it so much she went off into uncontrolled spasms of mirth. Kenny endured the quivering bed for a long time until it got too much. He bounced out of it and grabbed his clothes. For the second time in forty-eight hours he stalked out of the flat.

He had walked about for an hour in the cold blustery night, fuming. Then he found that he had left his flat key ring behind and spent another hour looking for a second key he had buried in the garden in a foolproof spot. With chattering teeth he drank several hot whiskeys and went to bed, but sleep eluded him. Towards dawn he slipped into a shallow dream in which there were a lot of sausages hiding under rashers from a German Flying Fork. But one of the sausages was his prick and it was having trouble appearing to be as natural as the other sausages all huddled together. Overhead the Flying Fork was escorted by two Messerschmidt nipples. An evil, guttural German voice came over the air. 'Nipple vun to Flying Fork. Enemy Wurstprick sighted. Avait instrukshuns to destroy protective rasher.' 'Flying Fork to Nipples vun and two. Go ahead.' The nipples zoomed down and his prick began to scream, 'No, no! I'm a sausage! I tell you, I'm a sausage! A neutral Irish sausage!' To no avail. With a crash the rasher was split apart by bullets. All the sausages wriggled away under other rashers leaving the prick exposed and squirming like a worm. Then it began to distend into a huge tottering erection, while he shouted at it, 'Get down, you bastard! Get down! Do you want to get us all killed?' He awoke, gasping for air, as the glittering prongs were streaking down. . . .

He was indeed gasping. He found he could hardly breathe. When he tried to clear his throat it was a dry rasp. He swore but nothing came. His voice was completely gone. At half-past eight he intercepted a neighbouring flatdweller and gave him written instructions to call his office. Then he crawled back into bed and dosed himself on aspirin and hot honey drinks. Something had gone wrong with the flat's central heating and he was very cold.

At twelve o'clock the door opened and Helga walked in.

'You forgot your key,' she said. 'I rang your office and they told me you were sick.' He opened and closed his mouth like a stranded fish. 'Have you lost your voice?'

Brilliant. That girl would go places. 'Can I get you anything?' He shook his head but she had turned to the door. 'There's a chemist next door.'

She brought him all sorts of things and then cooked him an omelette. He felt powerless. He wanted to tell her that she had herself to blame for all this, but as she handed him things all he could do was abjectly nod his thanks. She seemed to forget at times that he could at least hear and went on with a lot of idiotic mime, looking at him inquiringly as she touched her thoat and made a face like she was swallowing gravel. He leant back in disgust and closed his eyes. Jesus Christ, Kenny, you do pick 'em.

At five she left for her classes but was back again at eight. She made him grog and had some herself. She soon got quite merry and her laughter began to sound like bilge water chuckling. He never thought he could hate anyone so much. Close to nine Phyllis Cronin arrived. She was a tall gawky girl who had been banged by most fellows in the office. Things went wrong with her, too. The last time Kenny was banging her in her own home her mother had arrived back unexpectedly and in the panic of dressing, *sans* mislaid underpants, he had jammed his foreskin in his zip. While the mother was wandering around the house calling, 'Phy-llis, are you ho-ome?' he was dancing around in agony trying to get his penis free. But now he clasped her hands in his and gazed up at her as though she were the very embodiment of romance. Helga, smiling her crooked smile, played her game and tut-tutted over him, patting his pillow and talking about him as though she had been nursing him for years.

'But he has himself to blame,' she confided to the wide-eyed girl for whom such facts about the grave Kenny were indeed news. 'Last night he insisted on dancing around the flat in the nude. I told him he'd catch cold.'

Kenny grinned at Phyllis and gestured to Helga, touching his forehead. But Phyllis was believing every word.

'How are you, my ho-ho-ho laughing lion?' Helga

smiled, leaning towards him.

Dancing in the nude, ho-ho-ho laughing lion! Would he ever live it down at the office? By the time Phyllis left Helga was almost planning the honeymoon.

Then it struck him that that was just what she *was* planning. A woman of genius! All this nonsense about the baby and her tubes was just a ploy to arouse his interest and concern. She was luring him into persuading her to marry *against* her will! Look at her now tidying up the place as though she already owned it. And preparing the couch for herself without as much as a by your leave. Perfidious woman! He made a fist at her and pointed to the door. 'Oh, shut up,' she said, shaking out a blanket. He subsided on the pillows. Had he said a word?

At two he was still awake, cold, feeling very sorry for himself. He saw himself as a ridiculous toy lion being kicked around the city by laughing urchins. All his dignity was gone. Or whatever he wanted to call his dignity. In her own corner Helga was sniffling. Suddenly he was sorry for both of them. He with his notions of freedom, she reaching out from some grim isolation of her own for a creature she could possess and love. Whatever they were after they were both in a bit of a mess right now. He cleared his throat and said, 'Helga?' It was only a whisper but she heard him. He heard her getting up, and then she was climbing into the bed beside him all rough and hairy in her sweater and jeans. She turned on her side and he hugged into her feeling that for the first time their touch was human, feeling her warmth. And he wasn't touching her at all. Her body was buried beneath layers of clothes, soft warming layers. There couldn't be enough of them. He closed his eyes. Tomorrow could take care of babies and tubes and sexual relationships. Now all he wanted was to sleep. Eventually he did. And so did she.

JOHN McGAHERN

Sierra Leone

'I suppose it won't be long now till your friend is here,' the barman said as he held the glass to the light after polishing.

'If it's not too wet,' I said.

'It's a bad evening,' he yawned, the rain drifting across the bandstand and small trees of Fairview Park to stream down the long window.

She showed hardly any signs of rain when she came, lifting the scarf from her black hair. 'You seemed to have escaped the wet,' the barman was all smiles as he greeted her.

'I'm afraid I was a bit extravagant and took a taxi,' she said in the rapid speech she used when she was nervous or simulating confusion to create an effect.

'What would you like?'

'Would a hot whiskey be too much trouble?'

'No trouble at all,' the barman smiled and lifted the electric kettle. I moved the table to make room for her in the corner of the varnished partition, beside the small coal fire in the grate. There was the sound of water boiling, and the scent of cloves and lemon. When I rose to go to the counter for the hot drink, the barman motioned that he would bring it over to the fire.

'The spoon is really to keep the glass from cracking,' I nodded toward the steaming glass in front of her on the table. It was a poor attempt to acknowledge the intimacy of the favour. For several months I had been frustrating all his attempts to get to know us, but we had picked Gaffneys because it was out of the way and we had to meet like thieves. Dublin was too small a city to give even our names away.

'This has just come,' I handed her the telegram as soon as the barman had resumed his polishing of the glasses. It was from my father, saying it was urgent I go home at once. She read it without speaking. 'What are you going to do?'

'I don't know. I suppose I'll have to go home.'

'It doesn't say *why.*'

'Of course not. He never gives room.'

'Is it likely to be serious?'

'No, but if I don't go there's the nagging that it may be.'

'What are you going to do then?'

'I suppose go,' I looked at her apprehensively.

'Then that's goodbye to our poor weekend,' she said.

We were the same age and had known each other casually for years. I had first met her with Jerry McCredy, a politician in his early fifties, who had a wife and family in the suburbs, and a reputation as a womanizer round the city; but by my time all the other women had disappeared. The black-haired Geraldine was with him everywhere, and he seemed to have fallen in love at last when old, even to the point of endangering his career. I had thought her young and lovely and wasted, but we didn't meet in any serious way till the night of the Cuban Crisis.

There was a general fever in the city that night, so quiet as to be almost unreal, the streets and faces hushed. I had been wandering from window to window in the area round Grafton Street. On every television set in the windows the Russian ships were still on course for Cuba. There was a growing air that we were walking in the last quiet evening of the world before it was all consumed by fire. 'It looks none too good.' I heard her quick laugh at my side as I stood staring at the ships moving silently across the screen.

'None too good,' I turned. 'Are you scared?'

'Of course I'm scared.'

'Do you know it's the first time we've ever met on our

own?' I said. 'Where's Jerry?'

'He's in Cork. At a meeting. One that a loose woman like myself can't appear at,' she laughed her quick provocative laugh.

'Why don't you come for a drink, then?'

'I'd love to. With the way things are I was even thinking of going in for one on my own.'

There was a stillness in the bar such as I had never known. People looked up from their drinks as each fresh news flash came on the set high in the corner, and it was with visible relief that they bent down again to the darkness of their pints.

'It's a real tester for that old chestnut about the Jesuit when he was asked what he'd do if he was playing cards at five minutes to midnight and was suddenly told that the world was to end at midnight,' I said as I took our drinks to a table in one of the far corners of the bar, out of sight of the screen.

'And what would *he* do?'

'He'd continue playing cards, of course, It's to show that all things are equal. It's only love that matters.'

'That's a fine old farce,' she lifted her glass.

'It's strange, how I've always wanted to ask you out, and that it should happen this way. I always thought you very beautiful.'

'Why did'nt you tell me?'

'You were with Jerry.'

'You should still have told me. I don't think Jerry ever minded the niceties very much when he was after a woman,' she laughed, and then added softly, 'Actually, I thought you disliked me.'

'Anyhow, we're here this night.'

'I know, but it's somehow hard to believe it.'

It was the stillness that was unreal, the comfortable sitting in chairs with drinks in our hands, the ships leaving a white wake behind them on the screen. We were in the condemned cell waiting for reprieve or execution, except that this time the whole world was the cell. There was nothing we could do. The withering would happen as simply as the turning of a light bulb on or off.

Her hair shone dark blue in the light. Her skin had the bloom of ripe fruit. The white teeth glittered when she smiled. We had struggled toward the best years; now they waited for us, and all was to be laid waste as we were about to enter on them. In the freedom of the fear I moved my face close to hers. Our lips met. I put my hand on hers.

'Is Jerry coming back tonight?'

'No.'

'Can I stay with you tonight?'

'If you want that,' her lips touched my face again.

'It's all I could wish for—except, maybe, a better time.'

'Why don't we go then?' she said softly.

We walked by the Green, closed and hushed within its railings, not talking much. When she said, 'I wonder what they're doing in the Pentagon as we walk these steps by the Green?' it seemed more part of the silence than any speech.

'It's probably just as well we can't know.'

'I hope they do something. It'd be such a waste. All this to go, and us too.'

'We'd be enough.'

There was a bicycle against the wall of the hallway when she turned the key, and it somehow made the stairs and lino-covered hallway more bare.

'It's the man's upstairs,' she nodded towards the bicycle. 'He works on the buses.'

The flat was small and untidy.

'I had always imagined Jerry kept you in more style,' I said idly.

'He doesn't keep me. I pay for this place. He always wanted me to move, but I would never give up my own place,' she said sharply, but she could not be harsh for long, and began to laugh. 'Anyhow he always leaves before morning. He has his breakfast in the other house'; and she switched off the light on the disodered bed and chairs and came into my arms. The night had been so tense and sudden that we had no desire except to lie in one another's arms, and as we kissed a last time before turning to seek our sleep she whispered, 'If you want me during the night, don't be afraid to wake me up.'

The Russian ships had stopped and were lying off Cuba, the radio told us as she made coffee on the small gas stove beside the sink in the corner of the room the next morning. The danger seemed about to pass. Again the world breathed, and it looked foolish to have believed it had ever been threatened.

Jerry was coming back from Cork that evening, and we agreed as we kissed to let this day go by without meeting, but to meet at five the next day in Gaffneys of Fairview.

The bicycle had gone from the hallway by the time I left. The morning met me as other damp cold Dublin mornings, the world almost restored already to the everyday. The rich uses we dreamed last night when it was threatened that we would put it to if spared were now forgotten, when again it lay all about us in such tedious abundance.

'Did Jerry notice or suspect anything?' I asked over the coal fire in Gaffneys when we met, both of us shy in our first meeting as separate persons after the intimacy of flesh.

'No. All he talked about was the Cuban business. Apparently they were just as scared. They stayed up drinking all night in the hotel. He just had a terrible hangover.'

That evening we went to my room and she was in a calm and quiet way, completely free with her body, offering it as a gift, completely open. With the firelight leaping on the walls of the locked room, I said, 'There's no Cuban business now. It is the first time, you and I,' but in my desire was too quick; 'I should have been able to wait,' but she took my face between her hands and drew it down. 'Don't worry. There will come a time soon enough when you won't have that trouble.'

'How did you first meet Jerry?' I asked to cover the silence that came.

'My father was mixed up in politics in a small way, and he was friendly with Jerry; and then my father died while I was at the convent in Eccles Street. Jerry seemed to do most of the arranging at the funeral. And then it seemed natural for him to take me out on those halfdays and Sundays that we were given free.'

'Did you know of his reputation?'

'Everybody did. It made him dangerous and attractive. And then one Saturday halfday we went to his flat in an attic off Baggot Street. He must have borrowed it for the occasion for I've never been in it since. I was foolish. I knew so little. I just thought you lay in bed with a man and that was all that happened. I remember it was raining. The flat was right in the roof, and there was the loud drumming of the rain all the time. That's how it began. And it's gone on from there ever since.'

She drew me toward her, in that full openness of desire, but she quickly rose, ' have to hurry. I have to meet Jerry at nine'; and the pattern of her thieving had been set.

Often when I saw her dress to leave, combing her hair in the big cane armchair, drawing the lipstick across her rich curving lips in the looking glass, I felt that she had come with stolen silver to the room. We had dined with that silver, and now that the meal was ended she was wiping and shining the silver anew, replacing it in the black jewel case to be taken out and used again in Jerry's bed or at his table, doubly soiled; and when I complained she said angrily, 'What about it? He doesn't know.'

'At least you and he aren't fouling up anybody.'

'What about his wife? You seem very moral of a sudden.'

'I'm sorry. I didn't mean it,' I apologized, but already the bloom had gone from the first careless fruits, and we felt the responsibility enter softly, but definitely, as any burden.

'Why can't you stay another hour?'

'I know what'd happen in one of those hours,' she said spiritedly, but the tone was affectionate and dreamy with, perhaps, the desire for children. 'I'd get pregnant as hell in one of those hours.'

'What should we do?'

'Maybe we should tell Jerry,' she said, and it was my turn to be alarmed.

'What would we tell him?'

The days of Jerry's profligacy were over. Not only had he grown jealous but violent. Not long before, hearing that she had been seen in a bar with a man and not being able to find her, he had taken a razor and slashed the dresses in her wardrobe to ribbons.

'We could tell him everything,' she said without conviction. 'That we want to be together.'

'He'd go berserk. You know that.'

'He's often said that the one thing he feels guilty about is having taken my young life. That we should have met when both of us were young.'

'That doesn't mean he'll think me the ideal man for the job,' I said. 'They say the world would be a better place if we looked at ourselves objectively and subjectively at others, but that's never the way the ball bounces.'

'Well, what are we to do?'

'By telling Jerry about us, you're just using one relationship to break up another. I think you should leave Jerry. Tell him that you just want to start up a life of your own.'

'But he'll know that there's someone.'

'That's his problem. You don't have to tell him. We can stay apart for a while. And then take up without any thieving or fear, like two free people.'

'I don't know,' she said as she put on her coat. 'And then after all that, if I found that you didn't want me, I'd be in a nice fix.'

'There'd be no fear of that. Where are you going tonight?'

'There's a dinner that a younger branch of the Party is giving. It's all right for me to go. They think it rather dashing of Jerry to appear with a young woman.'

'I'm not so sure. Young people don't like to see themselves caricatured either.'

'Anyhow I'm going,' she said.

'Will it be five in Gaffneys tomorrow?'

'At five, then,' I heard as the door opened and softly closed.

'Does Jerry suspect at all?' I asked her again another evening over Gaffneys' small coal fire.

'No. Not at all. Odd that he often was suspicious when nothing at all was going on and now that there is he suspects nothing. Only the other day he was asking about you. He was wondering what had become of you. It seemed so long since we had seen you last.'

Our easy thieving that was hardly loving, anxiety curbed by caution, appetite so luxuriously satisfied that it could poorly give way to the dreaming that draws us close to danger, was wearing itself naturally away when a different relationship was made alarmingly possible. Jerry was suddenly offered a lucrative contract to found a new radio/television network in Sierra Leone, and he was thinking of accepting. Ireland as a small nation with a history of oppression was suddenly becoming useful in the Third World.

'He goes to London the weekend after next for the interview and he'll almost certainly take it.'

'That means the end of his political career here.'

'There's not much further he can get here. It gives him prestige, a different platform, and a lot of cash.'

'How do you fit into this?'

'I don't know.'

'Does he want to take you with him?'

'He'll go out on his own first. but he says that as soon as he's settled there and sees the state of play that he wants me to follow him.'

'What'll you do?'

'I don't know,' she said in a voice that implied that I was

now part of these circumstances.

Slane was a lovely old village in the English style close to Dublin. One Sunday we had lunch at the one hotel, more like avillage inn than a hotel, plain wooden tables and chairs, the walls and fireplaces simple black and white, iron scrapers on the steps outside the entrance; and she suggested that we go there the weekend Jerry was on interview in London. The country weekend, the walks along the wooded banks of the river, coming back to the hotel with sharp appetites to have one drink in the bar and then to linger over lunch, in the knowledge that we had the whole long curtained afternoon spread before us, was dream enough. But was it to be all that simple? Did we know one another at all, outside these carnal pleasures that we shared, and were we prepared to spend our lives together in the good or nightmare they might bring? And it was growing clearer that she wasn't sure of me and that I wasn't sure. So when the telegram came from the country I was for once almost glad of the usual drama and mysteriousness.

'Then that's goodbye to our poor weekend,' she handed me back the telegram in Gaffneys.

'It's only one weekend,' I protested. 'We'll have as many as we want once Jerry goes.'

'You remember when I wanted to tell Jerry that we were in love you wouldn't have it. You said we didn't know one another well enough, and then when we can have two whole days together you get this telegram. How are we ever going to get to know one another except by being together?'

'Maybe we can still go?'

'No. Not if you are doubtful. I think you should go home.'

'Will you come back with me this evening?'

'No. I have to have dinner with Jerry.'
'When?'
'At eight.'
'We'll have time. We can take a taxi.'
'No, love,' she was quite definite.
'Will you meet me when I come back, then?' I asked uncertainly.
'Jerry comes back from London on Sunday.'
'On Monday, then?'
'All right, on the Monday.' There was no need to say where or when. She even said, 'See you Monday,' to the barman's silent inquiry as we left, and he waved 'Have a nice weekend,' as he gathered in our glasses.

I was returning home: a last look at the telegram before throwing it away—an overnight bag, the ticket, the train—the old wheel turned and turned anew, wearing my life away; but if it wasn't this wheel it would be another.

Rose, my stepmother, seemed glad to see me, smiling hard, speaking rapidly. 'We even thought you might come on the late train last night. We said he might very well be on that train when we heard it pass. We kept the kettle on till after the news, and then we said you'll hardly come now, but even then we didn't go to bed till we were certain you'd not come.'
'Is there something wrong?'
'No. There's nothing wrong.'
'What does he want me for?'
'I suppose he wants to see you. I didn't know there was anything special, but he's been worrying or brooding lately. I'm sure he'll tell you himself. And now you'll be wanting something to eat. He's not been himself lately,' she added conspiratorially. 'If you can, go with him. do your best to humour him.'

We shook hands when he came, but we did not speak, and Rose and myself carried the burden of the conservation during the meal. Suddenly, as we rose at the end of the meal, he said, 'I want you to walk over with me and look at the walnuts.'

'Why the walnuts?'

'He's thinking of selling the walnut trees,' Rose said. They've offered a great price. It's for the veneer, but I said you wouldn't want us to sell.'

'A lot you'd know about that,' he said to her in a half-snarl, but she covertly winked at me, and we left it that way.

'Was the telegram about the selling of the walnut trees, then?' I asked as we walked together toward the plantation. 'Sell anything you want as far as I'm concerned.'

'No. I have no intention of selling the walnuts. I threaten to sell them from time to time, just to stir things up. She's fond of those damned walnuts. I just mentioned it as an excuse to get out. We can talk in peace here,' he said, and I waited.

'You know about this Act they're bringing in?' he began ponderously.

'No.'

'They're giving it its first reading, but it's not the law yet.'

'What is this Act?'

'It's an Act that makes sure that the widow gets so much of a man's property as makes no difference after he's dead—whether *he* likes it or not.'

'What's this got to do with us?'

'You can't be that thick. I'll not live forever. After this Act who'll get this place? Now do you get my drift? Rose will. And who'll Rose give it to? Those damned relatives will be swarming all over this place before I'm even cold.'

'How do you know that?' I was asking questions now simply to gain time to think.

'How do I know?' he said with manic grievance. 'Already the place is disappearing fast beneath our feet. Only a few weeks back the tractor was missing. Her damned nephew had it. Without as much as by my leave. They forgot to inform me. And she never goes near them that there's not something missing from the house.'

'That's hardly fair. It's usual to share things round in the country. She always brought more back than she took.'

I remembered the baskets of raspberries and plums she used to bring back from their mountain farms.

'That's right. Don't take my word,' he shouted. 'Soon you'll know.'

'But what's this got to do with the telegram?' I asked, and he quietened.

'I was in to see Callon the solicitor. That's why I sent the telegram. If I transfer the place to you obefore that Act becomes law, then the Act can't touch us. Do you get me now?'

I did—too well. He would disinherit Rose by signing the place over to me. I would inherit both Rose and the place if he died.

'You won't have it signed over to you, then?'

'No. I won't. Have you said any of this to Rose?'

'Of course I haven't. Do you take me for a fool or something? Are you saying to me for the last time that you won't take it?' And when I wouldn't answer he said with great bittermess, 'I should have known. You don't even have respect for your own blood,' and muttering, walked away toward the cattle gathered between the stone wall and the first of the walnut trees. Once or twice he moved as if he might turn back. but he did not. We did not speak any common language, and to learn another's language is more difficult than to learn any foreign language, especially since its perfect knowledge is sure to end in murder.

We avoided each other that evening, the tension making us prisoners of every small movement, and the next day I tried to slip quietly away.

'Is it going you are?' Rose said sharply when she saw me about to leave.

'That's right, Rose?'

'You shouldn't pass any heed on your father. You should let it go with him. He won't change his ways now. You're worse than he is, not to let it go with him.'

For a moment I wanted to ask her, 'Do you know that he wanted to leave you at my sweet mercy after his death?' but I knew she would answer, 'What does that matter? You know he gets these ideas. You should let it go with him'; and when I said 'Goodbye, Rose,' she did not answer, and I did not look back.

As the train trundled across the bridges into Dublin and by the grey back of Croke Park, all I could do was stare. The weekend was over like a life. If it had happened differently it would still be over. Differently we would have had our walks and drinks, made love in the curtained rooms, experimented in the ways of love, pretending we were taming instinct, imagining we were getting more out of it than had been intended, and afterwards. . . . Where were we to go from there, our pleasure now its grinning head. And it would be over and not over. I had gone home instead, a grotesquerie of other homegoings, and it too was over now.

She would have met him at the airport, they would have had dinner, and if their evenings remained the same as when I used to meet them together they would now be having drinks in some bar. As the train came slowly into Amiens Street, I suddenly wanted to find them, to see us all together. They were not in any of the Grafton Street bars, and I was on the point of giving up the impulse—with gratitude that I hadn't been able to fulfil it—when I found them in a hotel lounge by the river. They were sitting at the counter, picking at a bowl of salted peanuts between their drinks. He seemed glad to see me, getting off his stool, 'I was just saying here how long it is since we last saw you,' in his remorseless slow voice, as if my coming might lighten an already heavy-hanging evening. He was so friendly that I could easily have asked him how his interview had gone, amid the profusion of my lies, forgetting that I wasn't supposed to know.

'I've just come from London. We've had dinner at the

airport,' he began to tell me all that I already knew.

'And will you take this job,' I asked after he had told me at length about the weekend, without any attempt to select between details, other than to put the whole lot in.

'It's all arranged. It'll be in the papers tomorrow. I leave in three weeks' time,' he said.

'Congratulations,' I proffered uneasily. 'But do you have any regrets about leaving?'

'No. None whatever. I've done my marching stint and speeching stint. Let the young do that now. It's my time to sit back. There comes a time of life when your grapefruit in the morning is important.'

'And will her ladyship go with you?'

'I'll see how the land lies first, and then she'll follow. And by the way,' he began to shake with laughter and gripped my arm so that it hurt, 'don't you think to get up to anything with her while I'm gone.'

'Now that you've put it into my head I might try my hand,' I looked for danger but he was only enjoying his own joke, shaking with laughter as he rose from the bar-stool. 'I better spend a penny on the strength of that.'

'That—was—mean,' she said without looking up.

'I suppose it was. I couldn't help it.'

'You knew we'd be round. It was mean.'

'Will you see me tomorrow?'

'What do you think?'

'Anyhow, I'll be there.'

'How did your weekend in the country go?' she asked sarcastically.

'It went as usual, nothing but the usual,' I echoed her own sarcasm.

McCredy was still laughing when he came back. 'I've just been thinking that you two should be the young couple, and me the uncle, and if you do decide to get up to something you must ask Uncle's dispensation first,' and he clapped me on the back.

'Well, I better start by asking now,' I said quickly in case my dismay would show, and he let out a bellow of helpless laughter. He must have been drinking, for he put arms round both of us, 'I just love you two young people,' and tears of laughter slipped from his eyes. 'Hi, barman, give us another round before I die.'

I sat inside the partition in Gaffneys the next evening as on all other evenings, the barman as usual polishing glasses, nobody but the two of us in the bar.

'Your friend seems a bit later than usual this evening,' he said.

'I don't think she'll come this evening,' I said, and he looked at me inquiringly. 'She went down the country for the weekend. She was doubtful if she'd get back.'

'I hope there's nothing wrong. . . .'

'No. Her mother is old. You know the way, I was making for the safety of the roomy clichés.

'That's the sadness. You don't know whether to look after them or your own life.'

Before any pain of her absence could begin to hang about the opening and closing doors as the early evening drinkers bustled in, I got up and left; and yet her absence was certainly less painful than the responsibility of a life together. But what then of love? Love flies out the window, I had heard them say.

'She'll not come now,' I said.

'No. It doesn't seem,' he said as he took my glass with a glance in which suspicion equalled exasperation.

We did not meet till several weeks later. We met in Grafton Street, close to where we had met the first night. A little nervously she agreed to come for a drink with me. She looked quite beautiful, a collar of dark fur pinned to her raincoat.

'Jerry's in Sierra Leone now,' she said when I brought the drinks.

'I know. I read it in the papers.'

'He rang me last night,' she said. 'He was in the house of a friend—a judge. I could hear music in the background. I think they were a bit tight. The judge insisted he speak to me too. He had an Oxford accent. Very posh. But apparently he's as black as the ace of spades,' she laughed. I could see that she treasured the wasteful call more than if it had been a gift of brilliant stones.

She began to tell me about Sierra Leone, its swamps and markets, the avocado and pineapple and cacao and banana trees, its crocodile-infested rivers. Jerry lived in a white-columned house with pillars on a hillside above the sea, and he had been given a chauffeur-driven Mercedes. She laughed when she told me that a native bride had to spend the first nine months of her marriage indoors so that she grew light-skinned.

'Will you be joining Jerry soon?' I asked.

'Soon. He knows enough people high up now to arrange it. They're getting the papers in order.'

'I don't suppose you'll come home with me tonight, then?'

'No,' there wasn't a hint of hesitation in the answer; difficulty and distance were obviously great restorers of the moral order. 'You must let me take you to dinner, then, before you leave. As old friends. No strings attached.' I smoothed. 'That'll be nice,' she said.

Out in Grafton Street we parted as easily as two leaves sent spinning apart by any sudden gust. All things begin in dreams, and it must be wonderful to have your mind full of a whole country like Sierra Leone before you go there and risk discovering that it might be your life.

Nothing seems ever ended except ourselves. On the eve of her departure for Sierra Leone, another telegram came from the country. There was nothing mysterious about it this time. Rose had died.

The overnight bag, the ticket, the train. . . .

The iron gate under the yew was open and the blinds of

the stone house at the end of the gravel were drawn. Her flower garden, inside the wooden gate in the low whitethorn hedge just before the house, had been freshly weeded and the coarse grass had been cut with shears. Who would tend the flowers now? I shook hands with everybody in the still house, including my father, who did not rise from the converted car chair.

I heard them go over and over what happened, as if by going over and over it they would return it to the every-day. 'Rose got up, put on the fire, left the breakfast ready, and went to let out the chickens. She had her hand on the latch coming in, when he heard this thump, and there she was lying, the door half-open.

I went into the room to look on her face. The face was over too. If she had been happy or unhappy it did not show now. Would she have been happier with another? Who knows the person another will find their happiness or unhappiness with? Enough to say thatweighed in this scale it makes little difference or all difference.

'Why don't you let it go with him,' I heard her voice. 'You know what he's like.' She had lived rooted in this one place and life, with this one man, like the black sally in the one hedge, as pliant as it is knobbed and gnarled, keeping close to the ground as it invades the darker corners of the meadows.

The coffin was taken in. The house was closed. I saw some of the mourners trample on the flowers as they waited in the front garden for her to be taken out. She was light on our shoulders.

Her people did not return to the house after the funeral. They had relinquished any hopes thay had to the land.

'We seem to have it all to ourselves,' I said to my father in the empty house. He gave me a venomous look but did not reply for long.

'Yes,' he said. 'Yes. We seem to have it all to ourselves. But where do we go from here?'

Not, anyhow, to Sierra Leone. For a moment I saw the tall colonial building on a hill above the sea, its white pillars, the cool of the veranda in the evening. . . . Maybe they were facing one another across a dinner table at this very moment, a servant removing the dishes.

Where now is Rose?

I see her come on a bicycle, a cane basket on the handlebars. The brakes mustn't be working for she has to jump off and run alongside the bicycle. Her face glows with happiness as she pulls away the newspaper that covers the basket. It is full of dark plums, and eggs wrapped in pieces of newspaper are packed here and there among the plums. Behind her there shivers an enormous breath of pure sky.

'I suppose we might as well try and stay put for a time,' I answered, and when he looked at me sharply I added, 'For the sake of my own peace. That is, until things settle a bit, and we can find our feet again, and think.'

HELEN LUCY BURKE

Trio

Two people, a man and a little boy, were walking quickly along the road. The man had a white stick in one hand. His other hand rested on the boy's shoulder. The boy, too, had a stick, or rather a staff. He was dressed in Scout's uniform. By the look on his face he seemed to be proud of the physical contact with the man, though from time to time to maintain it he had to take a few steps at a jog-trot. He kept up a steady stream of talk to which the man replied at random.

About a hundred yards before the crossroads the repair gang had been at work. Even before they came to the rough place, the man slowed down and began to pat left and right with his stick.

'How did you know the repairs were there?' asked the boy.

'By the sound, by the sound,' said the man, smiling.

'But they don't make any sound.'

'We make it for them,' said the man.

The little boy could make no sense of the reply, and felt the man was making fun of him.

'Close your eyes and listen the next time,' explained the man who sensed the boy's hurt. 'You'll hear your steps getting dull and thumpy.'

It was a mid-afternoon in the end of April. The wind seemed soft but had a concealed edge. When they came to the turning the man let go the boy's shoulder and turned up the collar of his coat. He stood still for a minute or so, with his shuttered face tilted towards the sky.

'It's a blue sky with bits of white,' said the boy importantly. 'Do you know what blue is?'

'Of course,' said the man. 'It's like this.' He whistled a snatch of melody, rather quick and dashing. 'And this is white.' This time the tune seemed to the boy to be very slow and winding.

'How could a tune be a colour?' asked the boy.

'How could it not?' replied the man. 'In that gate, now, and up the drive, and mind you don't trip yourself up on the stone sill.'

As they went through the gate the boy stumbled on the ledge and felt resentfully that the blind man must be laughing at him. Dead leaves from several winters clogged the edges of the drive. He shuffled his feet through them, making a crackling noise like cornflakes. It was a long walk for a shilling, and there would be the calling back for Mr. Garvey and leaving him to his own house. All the same, he knew it would look good on the report sheet for the Scoutmaster. None of the other fellows would have done anything as charitable or romantic. It was his mother who had suggested it.

'Does your sister walk you here every Saturday just to listen to Miss Moone's gramophone?'

'My sister is a very kind woman to her brother.'

The boy worked this statement out in silence for a minute.

'You must be terrible fond of music,' he said politely. 'They play us music at school sometimes, but it often hasn't any tune at all. I don't call that music. It's just made-up.'

'Ah, that's the best kind,' said Garvey. 'You can fit your own tune to it.'

'Why wouldn't you just turn on the radio?'

'You don't hear chamber-music on the radio,' the man replied absently, 'and anyway she has stereo, which makes all the difference.'

They came round a bend among the trees and the house loomed over them. The man knocked on the door in a knowing-he-was-expected sort of way. Fumbling in his pocket he produced a coin.

'Oh, no,' protested the little boy, shocked. 'It's a shilling, you know, only, a Bob a Job, and I can't take it until I've fully finished and brought you home again. That's the rule.'

The door swung back. In the opening Miss Moone loomed like a tree. Her waving arms of welcome were tossing branches, her body the trunk of a fir.

The boy got well back behind his companion. He knew Miss Moone, not only because she often halted her cavalry-dash progress into the shops to talk to his mother, but also because several times he had formed part of the yapping band who followed her about shouting 'Big Miss Moone, Ticky tacky toon, Is it cold up in the sky? Reach me down a star.' Now and then she lashed out with her walking-stick at her tormentors. Mostly though she either went on as if she heard nothing, or else just turned and gave them the sort of look that would be pitiful and pleading in a woman half her bulk, but made Miss Moone look like a bullock in the slaughteryard.

'This is Edward.' said the blind man. 'I'm his good deed. Hetty wasn't able to bring me and the road is up along by the cross, so . . .' He tapped with his stick and laughed. 'Edward will call for me about six o'clock.'

He turned around to Eddie (And how did he know where I was standing? wondered the boy) and gave him a slight slap on the shoulder. It might have been a thank-you or it could have been in joke. The door closed. Through the panes in the upper half he saw the two going up the wide staircase towards Miss Moone's drawing-room, the angles of her figure as clearly defined as a handful of forks through the waves of dimpled glass.

A few drops of rain began to fall as a mat of white fleece swept across the pale yellow face of the sun. Suddenly tired of being a Scout the boy decided to try being an Indian. On soundless moccasined feet he flitted through the deep groves. The hawk-eyes were keen and watchful. No leaf bent. No twig cracked. But the game was quickly discarded as useless. The deserted garden with its unmown grass washing up about the pedestals of the cracked statues could not present even an imaginary hazard without which the game could not be sustained.

From an upstairs room of the square stone house, through an open window a branch of music blossomed.

'Blue and white,' muttered the little boy, shaking his head from side to side in bewilderment. He trotted cautiously to the foot of a chestnut tree which leaned in towards the open window. A stiff mat of thorn and grass provided a hiding-place for his staff. Spitting on his hands he began a struggling climb up the smooth-muscled trunk into the tangle of branches.

'Oh, how I love this early Spring sun,' cried Miss Moone. She led Garvey to a seat on the couch and pressed him into its chintzy depths.

Huge overblown roses on a yellowish background that had once been white. Her dear mother's choice. For a second she admired the splay of her hand against his shoulder, the fingers long and sensitive, the nails well-turned, oh the Moones had always good hands for the old blood showed! Then to provide an excuse for the lingering touch she nudged him gently sideways to where the pool of sunshine poured itself in a shaft of shivering gold on the arm of the couch.

'Feel the heat. Can you feel it, can you feel it?' Her voice had become a serious clarinet as she thought about her own thoughtfulness. For of course blind people are more sensitive to all influences on the remaining senses.

And there to prove it, Garvey was basking in the sunlight like a cat, with such twists and wriggles as if he were stroking himself against it. From far back in infancy he could remember a genial presence that beat against his eyelids, turning even *his* darkness to a warm red, before that vestige, too, had faded. But even yet, by tilting his face to a shadowed sky, he could say to his sighted companions, 'There it is: the sun,' and be more sure than they were.

'A nice, nice, sunshiny room,' he drawled, stretching out

his legs and giving the feet a little pirouette like the beginning of a ballet figure. 'And now, some suitable music?' In a reflective manner he added, 'We had the Bartok last week.'

Miss Moone recalled, as she invariably did, some details from a book in her father's library, telling how blind girls in China were urged into prostitution, the loss of power in one of the senses increasing the voltage in the others. And men?

This alien fifty per cent of her own race seemed to Miss Moone to be composed of beings unmoved by the fates which affected women. Even her father had appeared to her to be of a different species, as if he had dropped from some other planet and acquired the rudiments of speech without penetrating to its heart. And yet, with all that, somehow in the presence of men she felt that it was *she* who was the intruder, the aborigine who lingered on into the culture of the invaders. Only Garvey, whom she saw every Saturday, who never saw her, seemed innocent of threat, perhaps only because his severe gaze turned always inwards had never seared her huge frame with the invariable mortifying quiver of (first) surprise, (then) laughter, which was dealt out to her by stranger males. Before, that is, they learned she was the rich Miss Moone.

Oh undoubtedly, she thought, Garvey was different; and you could never guess by the quietness of him that he was a man at all. She searched her mind for some delicacy of action that would show him he was with a finer soul than the common run, for she felt that he had a sensitive face with the traces of hurt on it. Boorish people would have offended him, even with well-meant sympathy. The thing for her to do was to offer him what he could enjoy without any allusion to what he lacked. The Beethoven A Minor Quartet? No, no, that was music to hear in ecstatic stillness. What she wanted was something knee-squeezing, a graceful joyous melody at the culmination of which she could drop a comradely hand on his thigh, confident that the gesture would not be misunderstood.

The Mozart Quintet — yes, that was it.

A flurry of clarinet notes replied conversationally to the strings as she threw herself down on the carpet in the pool of sunshine.

'It's just the right kind of music for this room and this time of year,' she murmured, softly as she thought. (Though in fact her murmur, coming from her huge frame, was like the drone of a bassoon.)

His face nodded up and down in reply. It had the wistful knowingness of a Gothic saint in weathered limestone. The eyes were bright blue, and except for a fixity of focus, seemed as capable of vision as her own. Not for him the dark glasses of a conventional blind man; they were only for those sightless horrors whose eyes had wheeled and turned in their heads until they looked like filmy poached eggs; she had seen many of them begging with boxes. And she herself had her own use for dark glasses; great octagonal ones she had for walking in town which rendered her completely invisible, she felt, all six feet three of muscle and bone that separated brindle head from heel; and the dark glasses also helped her hearing into deafness so that she could not hear the catcalls or the muttered jokes.

'The stereo is wonderful,' said Garvey in the pause between the movements. 'We might have them sitting here with us. De Bavier,' he added vaguely, gesturing towards the end of the couch as if the soloist were sitting there.

Miss Moone gave her attention to the music which was rippling through the room in competition with the song of a blackbird who was proclaiming that the chestnut tree and the nest midway up belonged to him, to him, and not the boy huddled in the fork of the tree.

'Do you think he quite had it there? There's another version that I had. . . .' Garvey shushed her to silence. He seemed to be inhaling the music through the pores of his skin, leaning slightly forward so that the sunlight fell on half of his head. It brightened the hair it touched to russet while the rest of his head was shadowed black.

Apologetic to his hostess, he said when the movement ended, 'I wanted to get that bit.' He whistled a few notes and patted his chest as if he had stored the melody there.

Oh the pity, oh the pity. Sighing to herself Miss Moone moved over beside the fire and began to remove her clothes. Her melancholy was more pronounced than usual, partly because it was Spring and partly because she had been shopping the previous day for a dressing-gown. As usual she had sought something pink and perhaps frilled, and as usual she had finished up in a man's shop buying a grey hairy thing 'for my brother. About the same size as me.'

The blouse, folded tidily, she hung beside the cherry-coloured cardigan over the back of the chair. She had moved out of the sunlight into the red of the fire. It burnt her shoulder as she stooped forward to unfasten the brassiere which she wore over a woollen vest. Without it, her breasts dropped suddenly and flattened themselves. Until she removed the vest her figure might have been a man's. In bare feet and wearing only a skirt she moved back across the room out of the warm redness into the lemony pallor, the thin April sunlight that had a sour edge of frost to it.

'This is beautiful,' said Garvey dreamily. A Bach cello suite was filling the room with dark sound.

To the boy in the tree it was a bewilderment. Hooting sounds going from high to low, that were supposed to be music, and that queer big woman doing rude things. Of course Mr. Garvey couldn't actually see the rude things so perhaps they didn't cou t, really. . . . She was bending herself forward and then suddenly drawing herself upright with a snap so that the two long triangular flaps of flesh which hung from each side of her chest tossed in the air. She was so close to Mr. Garvey that if he had reached his hand out into the air the flaps would hit him. But Mr. Garvey was lying back in the depths of the couch, wearing an expression of great peace on his face though his eyes were wide open and glinting in blue flashes where the light struck them. And now Miss Moone had her back to the window so that Eddie could not make out well what she was at, except that it made him feel all embarrassed like reading those bits out of Bible in class, and wanting to look away, or feeling he ought to, and not being able. Her back was a funny colour, he noticed, and the skin was all slack like the way balloons got when they were left over after Christmas, with little puckered marks and a way the eye had of knowing that they would be unpleasant to the touch. When you poked at them the dent stayed in the surface; his grandmother had been able to do that with her feet before she died. And Miss Moone's back had red marks over it as well. And now, Janey, she was running around the room, in and out between the furniture.

In her own mind she was clothed only in light, on Mount Ida. A Bacchante, a Maenad, a tree-nymph, released every Saturday from the spell of enchantment that held her prisoner to respectability and a jumper and skirt.

She circled the room at a dizzying pace. Oh if Mr. Garvey only had eyes and thank God he had not! These Saturdays were all she had to remind her that she was a woman.

'Do you think we could have Haydn? The one we had last week?' asked Garvey. The Bach had frisked to a close.

Miss Moone sped on soundless feet to the chair near the window and paused for breath before answering.

'Oh that Bach. It's like tearing yourself away from Heaven. Yes, of course, I'll get the Haydn.'

The trembling of fatigue in her voice could easily be put down to musical emotion. A very creditable weakness.

Edward craned forward from his perch in the tree. He thought of certain cryptic statements made by his teacher during religious instruction. They began to make sense. Surely indeed something so ugly must be a sin, for surely God had never intended a woman to take up postures like this, whether anyone could see her or not. This lace shawl now — it was even worse than the skin!

Wrapping the folds around her Miss Moone thought of wedding days. It was in fact her mother's combing-jacket. Through its flower pattern her flesh shone pink-beige, and in her ears rang, not Haydn but nuptial music; and as she minced along the carpet a spectral groom, six feet six inches tall, supported her with his arm.

A celadon bowl, filled with narcissi stood on the corner table. She glided to it, buried her face in the flowers for refreshment, took them from the water and held them to her breast. This was the way she would have stood; these the flowers to sustain her through the ceremony with their dreamy breath; there on the couch was the groom she should have had.

'Ah Miss Moone, I can't think why, but this music makes me think of weddings and flowers and happy spring things. Lambs, birds' nests, tender young girls. . . .' His voice trailed away in a dreamy diminuendo.

He had turned his thin face to where Miss Moone was stealthily replacing the flowers in their vase. Once more Garvey had surprised her, for she could have sworn that she made no sound in leaving her place. With awe she remembered the uncanny sense of hearing possessed by the blind, for they can sense you in the far corner of a room by your heartbeats, a peculiar faculty like that of a mosquito for detecting the presence of a blood-bearer. In haste she began to clothe her torso again, as the Angelus rang out from the nearby Roman Catholic church.

Ten minutes later she was conducting Garvey decorously downstairs to where the little boy scout waited in the porch.

The two went down the path together. Neither spoke until they were out the gate. Then the boy asked, 'Is Miss Moone a good lady?'

'She is very good,' said Garvey. 'She is good to me and she is good to Miss Moone. And isn't that good enough for anyone?'

He had a queer kind of curly smile on his face, the boy noticed, and suddenly knew that Garvey did not need to be told a word about Miss Moone, not one single word, no more than if he and not Eddie had been sitting in the tree, no more than if he had eyes like the boy in the Grimm's fairy-story who could see through ten layers of bandages and split stones open with the keenness of his glance.

FRANK O'CONNOR

News for the Church

When Father Cassidy drew back the shutter of the confessional he was a little surprised at the appearance of the girl at the other side of the grille. It was dark in the box but he could see she was young, of medium height and build, with a face that was full of animation and charm. What struck him most was the long pale slightly freckled cheeks, pinned high up behind the grey-blue eyes, giving them a curiously oriental slant.

She wasn't a girl from the town, for he knew most of these by sight and many of them by something more, being notoriously an easygoing confessor. The other priests said that one of these days he'd give up hearing confessions altogether on the ground that there was no such thing as sin and that even if there was it didn't matter. This was part and parcel of his exceedingly angular character, for though he was kind enough to individual sinners, his mind was full of obscure abstract hatreds. He hated England; he hated the Irish Government, and he particularly hated the middle classes, though so far as anyone knew none of them had ever done him the least bit of harm. He was a heavy-built man, slow-moving and slow-thinking with no neck and a Punchinello chin, a sour wine-coloured face, pouting crimson lips, and small blue hot-tempered eyes.

'Well, my child,' he grunted in a slow and mournful voice that sounded for all the world as if he had pebbles in his mouth, 'how long is it since your last confession?'

'A week, Father,' she replied in a clear firm voice. It surprised him a little, for though she didn't look like one of the tough shots, neither did she look like the sort of girl who goes to confession every week. But with women you could never tell. They were all contrary, saints and sinners.

'And what sins did you commit since then?' he asked encouragingly.

'I told lies, Father.'

'Anything else?'

'I used bad language, Father.'

'I'm surprised at you,' he said with mock seriousness. 'An educated girl with the whole of the English language at your disposal! What sort of bad language?'

'I used the Holy Name, Father.'

'Ach,' he said with a frown, 'you ought to know better than that. There's no great harm in damning and blasting but blasphemy is a different thing. To tell you the truth,' he added, being a man of great natural honesty, 'there isn't much harm in using the Holy Name either. Most of the time there's no intentional blasphemy but at the same time it coarsens the character. It's all the little temptations we don't indulge in that give us true refinement. Anything else?'

'I was tight, Father.'

'Hm,' he grunted. This was rather more the sort of girl he had imagined her to be; plenty of devilment but no real badness. He liked her bold and candid manner. There was no hedging or false modesty about her as about most of his women penitents. 'When you say you were "tight" do you mean you were just merry or what?'

'Well, I mean I passed out,' she replied candidly with a shrug.

'I don't call that "tight", you know,' he said sternly. 'I call that beastly drunk. Are you often tight?'

'I'm a teacher in a convent school so I don't get much chance,' she replied ruefully.

'In a convent school?' he echoed with new interest. Convent schools and nuns were another of his phobias; he said they were turning the women of the country into imbeciles. 'Are you on holidays now?'

'Yes. I'm on my way home.'

'You don't live here then?'

'No, down the country.'

'And is it the convent that drives you to drink?' he asked with an air of unshakable gravity.

'Well,' she replied archly, 'you know what nuns are.'

'I do,' he agreed in a mournful voice while he smiled at her through the grille. 'Do you drink with your parents' knowledg added anxiously.

'Oh, yes. Mummy is dead but Daddy doesn't mind. He lets us take a drink with him.'

'Does he do that on principle or because he's afraid of you?' the priest asked dryly.

'Ah, I suppose a little of both,' she answered gaily, responding to his queer dry humour. It wasn't often that women did, and he began to like this one a lot.

'Is your mother long dead?' he asked sympathetically.

'Seven years,' she replied, and he realised that she couldn't have been much more than a child at the time and had grown up without a mother's advice and care. Having worshipped his own mother, he was always sorry for people like that.

'Mind you,' he said paternally, his hands joined on his fat belly, 'I don't want you to think there's any harm in a drop of drink. I take it myself. But I wouldn't make a habit of it if I were you. You see, it's all very well for old jossers like me that have the worst of their temptations behind them, but yours are all ahead and drink is a thing that grows on you. You need never be afraid of going wrong if you remember that your mother may be watching you from heaven.'

'Thanks, Father,' she said, and he saw at once that his gruff appeal had touched some deep and genuine spring of feeling in her. 'I'll cut it out altogether.'

'You know, I think I would,' he said gravely, letting his eyes rest on her for a moment. 'You're an intelligent girl. You can get all the excitement you want out of life without that. What else?'

'I had bad thoughts, Father.'

'Ach,' he said regretfully, 'we all have them. Did you indulge them?'

'Yes, Father.'

'Have you a boy?'

'Not a regular: just a couple of fellows hanging round.'

'Ah, that's worse than none at all,' he said crossly. 'You ought to have a boy of your own. I know there's old cranks that will tell you different, but sure, that's plain foolishness. Those things are only fancies, and the best cure for them is something real. Anything else?'

There was a moment's hesitation before she replied but it was enough to prepare him for what was coming.

'I had carnal intercourse with a man, Father,' she said quietly and deliberately.

'You what?' he cried, turning on her incredulously. 'You had carnal intercourse with a man? At your age?'

'I know,' she said with a look of distress. 'It's awful.'

'It is awful,' he replied slowly and solemnly. 'And how often did it take place?'

'Once, Father — I mean twice, but on the same occasion.'

'Was it a married man?' he asked, frowning.

'No, Father, single. At least I think he was single,' she added with sudden doubt.

'You had carnal intercourse with a man,' he said accusingly, 'and you don't know if he was married or single!'

'I assumed he was single,' she said with real distress. 'He was the last time I met him but, of course, that was five years ago.'

'Five years ago? But you must have been only a child then.'

'That's all, of course,' she admitted. 'He was courting my sister, Kate, but she wouldn't have him. She was running round with her present husband at the time and she only kept him on a string for amusement. I knew that and I hated her because he was always so nice to me. He was the only one that came to the house who treated me like a grown-up. But I was only fourteen, and I suppose he thought I was too young for him.'

'And were you?' Father Cassidy asked ironically. For some reason he had the idea that this young lady had no proper idea of the enormity of her sin and he didn't like it.

'I suppose so,' she replied modestly. 'But I used to feel awful, being sent up to bed and leaving him downstairs with Kate when I knew she didn't care for him. And then when I met him again the whole thing came back. I sort of went all soft inside. It's never the same with another fellow as it is with the first fellow you fall for. It's exactly as if he had some sort of hold over you.'

'If you were fourteen at the time,' said Father Cassidy, setting aside the obvious invitation to discuss the power of first love, 'you're only nineteen now.'

'That's all.'

'And do you know,' he went on broodingly, 'that unless you can break yourself of this terrible vice once for all it'll go on like that till you're fifty?'

'I suppose so,' she said doubtfully, but he saw that she didn't suppose anything of the kind.

'You suppose so!' he snorted angrily. 'I'm telling you so. And what's more,' he went on, speaking with all the earnestness at his command, 'it won't be just one man but dozens of men, and it won't be decent men but whatever low class pups you can find who'll take advantage of you — the same horrible, mortal sin, week in week out till you're an old woman.'

'Ah, still, I don't know,' she said eagerly, hunching her shoulders ingratiatingly, 'I think people do it as much from curiosity as anything else.'

'Curiosity?' he repeated in bewilderment.

'Ah, you know what I mean,' she said with a touch of impatience. 'People make such a mystery of it!'

'And what do you think they should do?' he asked ironically. 'Publish it in the papers?'

'Well, God knows, 'twould be better than the way some

of them go on,' she said in a rush. 'Take my sister Kate, for instance. I admit she's a couple of years older than me and she brought me up and all the rest of it, but in spite of that we were always good friends. She showed me her love letters and I showed her mine. I mean, we discussed things as equals, but ever since that girl got married you'd hardly recognise her. She talks to no one only other married women, and they get in a huddle in a corner and whisper, whisper, whisper, and the moment you come into the room they begin to talk about the weather, exactly as if you were a blooming kid! I mean you can't help feeling 'tis something extraordinary.'

'Don't you try and tell me anything about immorality,' said Father Cassidy angrily. 'I know all about it already. It may begin as curiosity but it ends as debauchery. There's no vice you could think of that gets a grip on you quicker and degrades you worse, and don't you make any mistake about it, young woman! Did this man say anything about marrying you?'

'I don't think so.' she replied thoughtfully, 'but of course that doesn't mean anything. He's an airy, light-hearted sort of fellow and it mightn't occur to him.'

'I never supposed it would,' said Father Cassidy grimly. 'Is he in a position to marry?'

'I suppose he must be since he wanted to marry Kate,' she replied with fading interest.

'And is your father the sort of man that can be trusted to talk to him?'

'Daddy?' she exclaimed aghast. 'But I don't want Daddy brought into it.'

'What you want, young woman,' said Father Cassidy with sudden exasperation, 'is beside the point. Are you prepared to talk to this man yourself?'

'I suppose so,' she said with a wondering smile. 'But about what?'

'About what?' repeated the priest angrily. 'About the little matter he so conveniently overlooked, of course.'

'You mean ask him to marry me?' she cried incredulously. 'But I don't want to marry him.'

Father Cassidy paused for a moment and looked at her anxiously through the grille. It was growing dark inside the church, and for one horrible moment he had the feeling that somebody was playing an elaborate and most tasteless joke on him.

'Do you mind telling me,' he inquired politely, 'am I mad or are you?'

'But I mean it, Father,' she said eagerly. 'It's all over and done with now. It's something I used to dream about, and it was grand, but you can't do a thing like that a second time.'

'You can't what?' he asked sternly.

'I mean, I suppose you can, really,' she said, waving her piously joined hands at him as if she were handcuffed, 'but you can't get back the magic of it. Terry is light-hearted and good natured, but I couldn't live with him. He's completely irresponsible.'

'And what do you think you are?' cried Father Cassidy, at the end of his patience. 'Have you thought of all the dangers you're running girl? If you have a child who'll give you work? If you have to leave this country to earn a living what's going to become of you? I tell you it's your bounden duty to marry this man if he can be got to marry you — which, let me tell you,' he added with a toss of his great head, 'I very much doubt.'

'To tell you the truth I doubt it myself,' she replied with a shrug that fully expressed her feelings about Terry and nearly drove Father Cassidy insane. He looked at her for a moment or two and then an incredible idea began to dawn on his bothered old brain. He sighed and covered his face with his hand.

'Tell me,' he asked in a far-away voice, 'when did this take place?'

'Last night, Father,' she said gently, almost as if she were glad to see him come to his senses again.

'My God,' he thought despairingly, 'I was right!'

'In town, was it?' he went on.

'Yes, Father. We met on the train coming down.'
'And where is he now?'
'He went home this morning, Father.'
'Why didn't you do the same?'
'I don't know, Father,' she replied doubtfully as though the question had now only struck herself for the first time.
'Why didn't you go home this morning?' he repeated angrily. 'What were you doing round town all day?'
'I suppose I was walking,' she replied uncertainly.
'And of course you didn't tell anyone?'
'I hadn't anyone to tell,' she said plaintively. 'Anyway,' she added with a shrug, 'it's not the sort of thing you can tell people.'
'No, of course,' said Father Cassidy. 'Only a priest,' he added grimly to himself. He saw now how he had been taken in. This little trollop, wandering about town in a daze of bliss, had to tell someone her secret, and he, a good natured old fool of sixty, had allowed her to use him as a confidant. A philosopher of sixty letting Eve, aged nineteen, tell him all about the apple! He could never live it down.
Then the fighting blood of the Cassidys began to warm in him. Oh, couldn't he, though? He had never tasted the apple himself, but he knew a few things about apples in general and that apple in particular that little Miss Eve wouldn't learn in a whole lifetime of apple-eating. Theory might have its drawbacks but there were times when it was better than practice. 'All right, my lass,' he thought grimly, 'we'll see which of us knows most!'
In a casual tone he began to ask her questions. They were rather intimate questions, such as a doctor or priest may ask, and, feeling broadminded and worldly-wise in her new experience, she answered courageously and straightforwardly, trying to suppress all signs of her embarrassment. It emerged only once or twice, in a brief pause before she replied. He stole a furtive look at her to see how she was taking it, and once more he couldn't withhold his admiration. But she couldn't keep it up. First

she grew uncomfortable and then alarmed, frowning and shaking herself in her clothes as if something were biting her. He grew graver and more personal. She didn't see his purpose; she only saw that he was stripping off veil after veil of romance, leaving her with nothing but a cold, sordid, cynical adventure like a bit of greasy meat on a plate.

'And what did he do next?' he asked.

'Ah,' she said in disgust, 'I didn't notice.'

'You didn't notice!' he repeated ironically.

'But does it make any difference?' she burst out despairingly, trying to pull the few shreds of illusion she had left more tightly about her.

'I presume you thought so when you came to confess it,' he replied sternly.

'But you're making it sound so beastly!' she wailed.

'And wasn't it?' he whispered, bending closer, lips pursed and brows raised. He had her now, he knew.

'Ah, it wasn't, Father,' she said earnestly. 'Honest to God it wasn't. At least at the time I didn't think it was.'

'No,' he said grimly, 'you thought it was a nice little story to run and tell your sister. You won't be in such a hurry to tell her now. Say an Act of Contrition.'

She said it.

'And for your penance say three Our Fathers and three Hail Marys.'

He knew that was hitting below the belt, but he couldn't resist the parting shot of a penance such as he might have given a child. He knew it would rankle in that fanciful little head of hers when all his other warnings were forgotten. Then he drew the shutter and didn't open the farther one. There was a noisy woman behind, groaning in an excess of contrition. The mere volume of sound told him it was drink. He felt he needed a breath of fresh air.

He went down the aisle creakily on his heavy policeman's feet and in the dusk walked up and down the path before the presbytery, head bowed, hands behind his back. He saw the girl come out and descend the steps under the massive fluted columns of the portico, a tiny, limp, dejected figure. As she reached the pavement she pulled herself together with a jaunty twitch of her shoulders and then collapsed again. The city lights went on and made globes of coloured light in the mist. As he returned to the church he suddenly began to chuckle, a fat good-natured chuckle, and as he passed the statue of St. Anne, patron of marriageable girls, he almost found himself giving her a wink.

TIM PAT COOGAN

The Compromise

The train stopped, in the middle of a rugby comment, jolting his mind out of the rut of deadening but therapeutic trivia and edged him back to the beach and the fond irritation of Billy's incessant questioning as he trotted along beside him, squeezing his hand, delighted to be out again at night, alone with his father.

'Daddy, why are there no people in swimming now? Too cold? We're not cold are we, daddy?'

'No, but we're walking, you see. If we were sitting down around a fire like those other people, we'd be cold now too. It's January you know. January is in winter.'

'But those people weren't sitting around a fire. They were swimming, weren't they, daddy?'

'They were swimming then, but they'd be sitting down around the fire afterwards.'

'Would they dress themselves then, daddy?'

His mind had somersaulted with desire at the recollection of the scene they had come on the previous year, but he forced himself to answer in the same expository tone, 'Yes, I suppose so. They were swimming with no clothes because it was dark, but when they'd be sitting around the fire they could see each other, so then they'd put on their clothes.'

'It's very rude to have no clothes on, isn't it, daddy? They should have put on their clothes, shouldn't they, daddy? That's where the fire was, wasn't it daddy?'

'Yes, that's where it was,' he answered and squeezed Billy's hand as they passed the spot where they'd come on the barbecue the previous August.

The moon had been shining then too, and it was possible to make out the forms of the swimmers in the water as they splashed and shrieked. He had begun to think sourly that he had never been at a barbecue like that. The one time they'd had one, Hilda had gone home in a huff because, to begin with, there hadn't been any other girls there. The girls had arrived later and everyone had a great time and another story went round the district about his wildness and his affair. The reality had been simply another row. But Billy was chattering on and it was necessary to change the subject.

'Billy, would you like to play football? Will I get you a football?'

The child skipped with delight, 'Oh boy, would I, would I, would I. You bet, That's great.'

And then running and twisting before them in the firelight they saw a boy and a girl. The boy was trying to force the girl towards the water and she was putting up a pretence of terror. Tussling and teasing, they came together for a moment stark naked and then the boy spun the girl around to give her a resounding spank on the bottom. Both broke into a run and the surf claimed them, smacking and shrieking with the joys of lust and youth on a warm summer's night.

He had walked on in a fog of envy and desire trying to stem his irritation at Billy's incessant questioning, and at the same time doing his best to placate him with enough innocuous information to prevent his spreading lurid stories amongst the neighbours. In August it had seemed important to prevent anyone outside the family from knowing the reason for the moonlit walks. Now they'd have to hear and, somehow, it didn't seem to matter a damn.

Nevertheless as he forced his mind back to his surroundings he could feel himself clutching his thighs through his trousers' pocket with the strain of thinking but not showing. He seemed to have drifted out to the edge of the others' conversation and with neither the opportunity nor the wish to join it, he looked out the window at the massed traffic passing along Lansdowne Road. When he had begun to commute, first to school and then to the rugby ground, almost twenty-five years ago now, the puffing-billy never halted except when there was a big match on. The few schoolchildren going to St. Conleth's in their green and black caps or the occasional widow making her way along the Dodder towards the Sweep were always able to use the wicket gate to enter the station and slip across the line on the pedestrian way, and the handful of cyclists and cars never seemed numerous enough to make it appear unreasonable that they should wait until the gates swung open behind the train. Nowadays, there seemed to be very few pedestrians, the cyclists had almost given way to scooters and Japanese motorcycles and the motor traffic, Mercedes, Cortinas and penile vehicles whose names he could never remember, roared along in such quantities as to make it appear almost unfair that the train should occasionally necessitate the closing of the gates to take passengers through the flood of traffic.

From his window he could see brass plaques outside most of the houses on both sides of the road. They were all offices now, or nearly so, 'Institutes', 'Federations', with here and there modern looking signs got up without any capital letters proclaiming that here So-and-so and So-and-so and 'Associates' carried on business in advertising, architecture and a new vague craft known as 'Consultants'.

When the crowds used to pour down onto it from the trams and buses on the main road above, often to see him play, the four-storey red-bricked houses had been all private dwellings and his present companions had been glad to know him. Now they only took the train because the traffic made it difficult for them to get parking places for their cars, whereas he did so because he couldn't afford a car. At most times of the year there never seemed much point in the others making any special effort to seek him out behind his paper. The day before an International was different, however. His views carried weight and there was even some kudos to be gained from sitting with him.

Brady wore a crombie and a silk scarf framed his port and sirloin jowls. At one stage he'd been a rival of his for a place in the Leinster pack, but he'd faded out at the provincial level and blended into his father's large firm of solicitors. Larger now, apparently, to judge from occasional references in the business sections of the newspapers to his being made a director of this firm or chairman of that society. O'Connor had just been appointed general manager of the new Celtic Insurance Company and was apparently responsible for the firm's million pound expansion into the property market; Murphy was something altitudinous in banking; O'Reilly a literary-minded accountant.

They differed in shape and size. O'Connor, thinner than Brady, had been a good social athlete in his day and was now çrew-cutted into a fit looking Harvard School of Business type mould. Murphy had kidney trouble, was slightly built, more diffident and institutionalised than the others. He remembered Murphy had once ten years ago dissuaded him from applying for a loan so discreetly and tactfully that he hadn't even brought up the subject of money by the time he walked out of Murphy's office, cheered by his friendly approach and enquiries after his family and slightly ashamed that he had bothered to take up his time at all with such a trivial matter.

O'Reilly was prematurely grey and was a distinguished looking figure at the first nights he attended in evening dress, and in his office to which he wore bow tie and a velvet jacket.

But there was a similarity about them. Apart from being clearly well-off, they all obviously belonged to the decision-taking echelon. Had it not been for the bad morning which had driven extra crowds onto the train and into their first class compartment, they would not have had to share it with the students, clerks, civil servants like himself and all the rest of the limbo men who chattered and fogged the windows and went into their work to be told what to do.

The proximity of the English match prompted O'Reilly to tell a story about a client of his from Belgium who had bought an estate for £200,000 and made an immediate profit because the British had devalued just as the sale was going through. O'Connor and Murphy nodded approvingly and prepared to contribute similar anecdotes when Brady brought him into the conversation again by saying with an air of considered judgement 'I don't think it was the best score ever seen at Lansdowne Road, but your try against England was the best score ever seen in an International.'

The others nodded in agreement, and in a sudden burst of recollected enthusiasm O'Connor abandoned an anecdote about a client who had made a killing on Tynagh Mines, on his advice, to say admiringly, 'You know I never realised that a wing forward could run so fast until you took off that time.'

'Jasus,' he said frankly, 'I didn't either!' There was a spontaneous burst of chatter and smiling reaction.

But even though he often reverted to it mentally or got some comfort when others did so in public, that triumph, too, had been flawed, a little like the barbecue he had arranged years ago where he got the credit and everyone else the enjoyment. The others began telling each other bits about the match and as the train pulled across the level crossing, past the grounds, he was able to see glimpses of the pitch where he had made his break into the record books.

He had been catching the English scrum-half regularly all through the match, greatly minimising the amount of possession they had been getting in the line outs and set pieces, and partly through his example and exhortation as pack leader the rest of the team had played above themselves also so as to keep the English lead down to two points with five minutes to go. However two points down in an International with your pack tiring and players tending to bog down on the half-way line is a formidable lead to overtake and the crowd, which up to that point had been surprised and delighted with the spirited Irish display, were just beginning to drift over to a group worry that the frequent Irish failing of a last minute fumble would occur, giving the British a final score which would transform the occasion from being a gallant Irish defeat to yet another clear-cut English win. And just at that moment there was a scrum just inside the English half.

He hadn't thought about anything but rugby since the game began, but tiring in strength and concentration, a wisp of upset crossed his mind and the thought of Hilda and his mother obtruded suddenly.

He tried to restore his concentration by standing up to give a last roar of encouragement to the pack before the English scrum-half put in the ball and it was only as he got down to push shoulder against the front row prop's buttocks, left arm automatically reaching out to clutch illegally at the English wing forward, that he realised that he had noticed the English full-back coming across behind the scrum on the blind side. In all probability the English were going to try a breakthrough with the full-back appearing unexpectedly to carry the ball through the Irish defence, luring the wing-threequarter out of place and then passing to Banfield Taylor, their Olympic sprinter and wing-threequarter.

England won the strike and he made for the full-back, hoping that if the scrum-half decided to initiate the run for it, the Irish back row would cover him off. But the scrum-half gathering the greasy ball hurriedly as it emerged sluggishly through the lock forward's legs, saw him coming and, a little unnerved by his earlier tackling, lofted his pass to the full-back so that it hung for an instant between the converging green and white shirts. Miraculously, the ball stuck to his fingers as he arched forward and away from the white figure of the Englishman who slipped as he tried to check his stride and catch him. There was nothing between him and the English line except fifty yards of grass. For about a second he was the only man in the ground who realised the enormity of this. The English attack continued its forward momentum behind him and the crowd was unresolved as to whether the scrum had formed correctly and might not be whistled down again by the referee.

Then there was mass realisation of what had happened. The ball was still in play and an Irish player was in possession of it heading for the English line. Behind him, the English wall of white turned back and broke into individual pursuits. The Irish team followed in their wake and the crowd exploded in a mass fusing of personality and aspiration to roar their fellow-Irishman on to success. As he ran, the roar both exalted and terrified him. Everything came back to him as he goaded himself on: opportunity, responsibility, resolution, the trio he could rarely master.

'Jesus,' he had sobbed, in his thunderous isolation 'your mother says you're useless, Hilda has nothing but contempt for you, you can't pass an exam — do something for once, do. . . .do. . . do. . . .'

As he passed the twenty-five yard line, a man in the crowd had suffered a heart attack, the death unnoticed as the rest of the crowd screamed him on with increasing hysteria as he neared the line. He had never felt such strain before or since; his heart in his throat, his chest raw, his legs plunging heavily. As he babbled out his crisis over his mother and Hilda, the incredible presumption of attempting to outrun Banfield Taylor began to dawn on him. Should he pass? He couldn't check his stride to look round for support. He was spurring himself on for the last few feet 'You mother. . . .fucking. . . . ' when Banfield Taylor tackled him from behind. Another English player hit him a second later and he lay for a moment, stunned and exhausted, with the ball trapped underneath his chest. Why hadn't he passed? He could do nothing right. He could hear his mother screaming at him quite clearly and see her mouthing, 'That dirty girl. If you marry her, you shit on your father's memory. That whore. . . . ' Why hadn't he passed? Then his head began to clear a little and he felt them thumping him on the back and became aware of the pain in his chest as they lifted him up and he discovered that he had fallen just over the line and won an historic victory.

It was ridiculously melodramatic. He and Banfield Taylor had to be carried off on stretchers. He with three ribs that had cracked from falling on the ball and Banfield Taylor with his nose and eyebrows badly gashed by one of his flailing studded boots.

As the two reeking gladiators were carried off through the thunderous crowd to the dressing rooms, he had been enveloped in a marvellous peace. All the ugly things hung emollient, cornerless, unhurtful in the aspic of his triumph. Hilda getting silent and cold when he told her what his mother had said. He knew she was upset over the baby. 'No matter what we feel for each other, they'll still say, "He had to marry her",' she said, but still he hadn't been able to understand the illogicality of their row. Her breaking it off, slamming the door of her parents' home in his face after telling him that he 'needn't bother keeping a ticket for the match. I wouldn'tdream of humiliating you by appearing with you in public'. But at that moment, he knew it would be all right. She was too generous not to be glad for his triumph. Probably on Monday he would get a phone call to the office and she would say, 'I'm sorry about the row,' and they would meet that night after the Novena. Everything was serene, but as the crowd roared out their ephemeral love for him, one of the few verses of poetry that stuck in his memory since school days came back to him. 'The Donkey':

I, too, had my one far, fierce hour and sweet,
For there were shouts about my head
And palms before my feet. . . .

One hour of sweetness about summed up his life, he

thought, and then he had to make an effort at carriage conversation, in response to a question from Brady.

'You're going to the match, of course?'

'No,' he said. 'I'm taking one of the kids down the country. Promised him a long time ago. It's all arranged. Can't get out of it now. It'd disappoint him. They're all expecting him. . . .'

He stopped. What in the name of Jesus was he making all the fucking excuses for? It was none of their fucking business. But, all the same, he felt himself blushing slightly. Murphy discreetly veered away from the subject. His banking discretion told him immediately that there was something somewhere not covered by a nine-to-five platitude.

'But sure, you'll hear it on the car radio.'

His embarrassment deepened. 'No, I don't drive. We're going by train.'

Jesus, why did he have to tell them that?

Brady laughed, 'Be God, it's no wonder you look so fit. The bloody car's a killer. No car, no worries, that's your secret.'

The others accepted Brady's cue with unanimity.

'Be God, you are sticking it well,' said O'Connor.

'You must be about the same weight now that you were then?' asked O'Reilly.

'I was thirteen-nine the day of the match. I'm fourteen-three now.'

That startled them—only eight pounds in eighteen years. The conversational seagulls rose from the rocks of convention and they stepped out at Westland Row in a flurry of, 'Ah, soft jobs,' 'No worries' and 'Easy livings'.

And he *was* fit looking. He took comfort from this fact as he passed himself in several shop windows and cheered up a little, encouraging his mind to work out of the fog of last night and towards more hopeful considerations. It had been on the tip of his tongue to say to Brady that 'soft jobs' were not as soft as he might imagine and that he had reason to expect that his own work would become more arduous and more responsible shortly. But he only had the office grapevine and his own intuition to go on, at the moment. However, usually these signs were sufficient to gauge promotional opportunities correctly and, from the beginning of the week, he had been confidently expecting to be called into the Secretary's office. If it did not come today, it seemed inevitable that it would come next week, probably on Monday or Tuesday.

It was to be today. The house-phone rang within a quarter of an hour of his sitting at his desk to summon him before O'Faolain, the Secretary of the Department. He had never liked O'Faolain. The touch of fanaticism in his furtherance of the Irish language, combined with a Kerry cuteness, made him too archetypal a figure of the successful Christian Brother moulded civil servant for his taste.

However a career Civil Servant who had reached the Principal Officer plateau early and stayed there late must not offend the Secretary of the Department if he wants to either reach the heights of an Assistant Secretaryship or even be allocated interesting work on the plateau. He had given up hope of the Secretarial posts but he hoped in recent months that this effort to please O'Faolain might result in his being appointed to a trade section which would mean making trips to London. But it turned out better than he had hoped. He was going up, not across, partly, O'Faolain indicated, because he had recommended him particularly. He was to become one of the two Assistant Secretaries to the new Department of Transport and Power that was being hived off from the Department of Industry and Commerce, in order to cope with the specular boom in the country's tourist trade. He and the other Assistant Secretary would rank joint second, under the Secretary himself, below the Minister in the pecking order.

'There's new ideas needed now. The country's moving ahead. Tourism is bringing in more now than the cattle industry. We have to be "with it", as the fella said. Ye'll have to travel and see how they do it in other countries and brief the Minister. Steve's not as young as he used to be.' And here, O'Faolain looked meaningfully at him.

He felt an almost insupportable thrill of pleasure for, while striving to tell himself that O'Faolain had probably told the other Assistant Secretary the same thing, he realised that Kelly was not of his calibre and that the Secretary of the Department had, at best, five years to go before retirement. Christ, what a vista that opened up. He almost staggered back to his desk.

But like every other triumph in his life it had not come at a moment of unadulterated joy. First he felt a thrill of pleasure that now Brady and the others would want to seek him out in the carriage all the year round, but it soon cooled and he realised that that sort of impulse was what had brought him into the Service in the first place—instead of taking the risk of becoming a journalist and perhaps, through journalism, becoming the writer he had once dreamed of being. Everything in his life appeared to come only as a balance to something bad, not as a straightforward gain the way other people seemed to win success. Like the time that Auntie had left him a thousand pounds and he discovered that Hilda had been writing cheques and he started drinking so that they had ended up far worse off than before he got the legacy. That had been in their abrasive days. Now they had more or less come to terms with each other.

If he hadn't loved her, perhaps he might have been a writer. He hadn't needed love for that. He should have found some docile creature who was good at money and would type his manuscripts.

I could not love thee, dear, so much
Loved I not honour more.

More schoolboy poetry. If he had wanted to be a writer that much neither poverty nor woman nor anything else would have deterred him. He never read anything new nowadays. What was the good, he had rationalised. Reading would only make him dissatisfied and he couldn't afford to become dissatisfied. You couldn't afford to find your work too boring when you'd a wife and children to support. A wife. Children. Fulfilment and deprivation. Heights and horrors. Now that he was successful, he could read again; ideas were permissible near the top.

The theatre, art galleries, places that got you a doubtful reputation for being a long-hair were now *de rigueur.* O'Faolain had expressly said that he'd be expected to be 'with it'.

He found a phone from one of the other desks so that he could ring Maurice without being overheard. Hilda had often sneered at him for not having an office of his own. Well, he'd have one now and she'd be proud of him again. He'd wait until tonight to tell her. He could imagine what she'd be like in bed, after hearing the news. That was Hilda. This morning he'd hated her and all the horror she'd put him through. Now he desired her and wished they were together in the dark, in bed.

While waiting for the switchboard to get Maurice's number, remembrance brought repugnance with desire. The night they both associated with Billy's conception. The moon shining on the bed, her white bottom wriggling with desire as she lay face downwards rolling off her black lace pants. She'd 'had the friend,' as she called it, and he could see the tip of the Southall appearing from the dark material of her pants like a white banana. He had fallen on her immediately to avoid seeing the stain. Desire overcame distaste and they did it backways. Not really backways, the way he had wanted to, but the way she wanted it, his tongue in her ear, his hands kneading her breasts as he pumped his seed into her womb. . . .God, if she'd done it his way everything might have been all right. . . .Billy should not have begun that night. In all probability he hadn't of course. With eight children it was hard to be sure about these things. Perhaps it had only been traces of a haemorrhage or she could have become pregnant later. In those days they had made love almost as often as they had fought. It was probably the combination of the moonlight and the effect of the moon on Billy that gave that particular bout a semi-guilty, almost superstitious association with his conception in their minds.

Maurice had said 'Hello' three times before he realised his brother-in-law was talking through his recollections.

'Oh! Maurice? Bill here. Are you going to the match tomorrow? . . .No, I don't want a ticket, I want to borrow the car if you're not using it. . . .Thanks very much. . . . No, I have to miss the match. . . .Yes, there's a problem. . . . Actually, Maurice, we're putting Billy in. . . .Sure, I know that. . . .Thanks, Maurice, you're very good. . . .No, there's no way out. . . .Mercy of God I got up last night to go to the jacks, I found him with Kathy—he'd the hand over her mouth, there was blood all over the pillow, he'd a breadknife. . . .No, no, she'll be alright, the doctor says her hair will cover the scar and she's too young to feel much shock. . ..No, not at all, Maurice, there's no need for you to come, I'll be able to manage myself, I'm buying him a football and he thinks we're going to the match. . . .Yes I know, Maurice, you're very good, thanks very much, I'll pick it up around twelve.'

After replacing the phone, he felt his upper lip trembling and the tears coming. He cried into his hands for a minute or so and then, not having a handkerchief, blew his nose into a piece of foolscap. As usual, Hilda hadn't given him a handkerchief, not having a handkerchief when he needed it inflamed some of his old angers against her. But after combing his hair, he felt better and he impulsively decided to ring her to tell her that Maurice was giving him the car. There was no need to but he always felt an urge to speak to her at moments of elation or crisis. His home number was engaged. Hilda was probably speaking to one of the group of housewives who phoned her each day to complain interminably about their problems. He smashed down the phone in fury. Christ! What sort of a wife was she? The house phone rang. It was O'Faolain again.

'There's just one little thing, now, we'd better keep the news of the changes to ourselves for a few days. D'ye mind not even tellin' the good lady? These things have to be done properly you know. We'll have to get a picture of ye, of yiz both and the Minister'll be announcin' the new Department in the Dail and the Government Information Bureau will be givin' out the pictures with your *curriculum vitae.* So it'll be another couple of weeks before we can go public, as it were. Shure y'don't mind holdin' on? Ah, that's the good soldier.'

'Not at all,' he answered, 'not at all. No problem. That'll be all right now. God bless.' He replaced the receiver and was about to tell Mrs. O'Shaughnessey that if Hilda rang she was to give her a message that Maurice was giving the car tomorrow and that he had gone out to buy Billy a football but he decided against it. Mention of Billy might prod Hilda into telling Mrs. O'Shaughnessey about his condition and it wouldn't do for a man with his potential of advancement to have people thinking that it was in any way hereditary or on his side of the family. That could be bad for a man nearing the top. He contented himself with saying that he'd be back in an hour and went out to buy Billy a football. 'A plastic one will do,' he told the shop assistant, 'it's just to keep a little boy quiet on a car journey.'

EDNA O'BRIEN

Ways

A narrow road and the first tentative fall of snow. A light fall that is merely preparatory and does not as yet make life cumbersome for the people or the herds. Around each clapboard house a belt of trees, and around the younger trees wooden Vs to protect the boughs from the heavier snow. The air is crisp and it is as if the countryside is suddenly miraculously revealed — each hill, each hedgerow, each tiny declivity more pronounced in the mantle of snow. Autumn dreaminess is over and winter is being ushered in.

The road could be anywhere. The little birches, the sound of a river, the humped steel bridge, the herds of cattle, the silo sheds, and the little ill-defined tracks suggest the backwardness of Ireland or Scotland or Wales. But in fact it is Vermont. Together they are braving the elements — two women in their thirties who have met for a day. Jane has lent Nell, her visitor, a cape, snow boots, and fuzzy socks. They pass a house where three chained guard dogs rear up in the air and bark so fiercely it seems as if they might break their fetters and come and devour the passers-by. Jane is a little ashamed; it is, after all, her neighbourhood, her Vermont, and she wants things to be perfect for Nell. She is glad of the snow and points proudly to the little pouches of it, like doves feathers, on a tree. She apologises for the dogs by saying that the poor man has a wife who has been mentally ill for twenty years and has no help in the house.

'In there?' Nell says.

'Yes, she's in there somewhere,' Jane says, and together they look at a little turret window with its second frame of fresh snow and a plate glass with a tint of blue in it. Together they say, 'Jane Eyre,' and think how odd to be telepathic, having only just met.

'You were wonderful last night,' Jane says.

'I was nervous,' Nell says.

'Ironing your dress, I guess I was, too. It was so delicate, I was so afraid.'

'Afraid?'

'That it might just disappear.'

Nell remembers the evening before — arriving from New York, going up to a cold bedroom and taking out a sheaf of poems she was going to read to the English Department of the university where Jane and her husband teach. Scrambling through her notes in the guest bedroom, searching anxiously for a spare refill for her pen, she was once again envisaging a terrible scene in which her head would be hacked off and would go rolling down the aisle between rows of patient people, while her obedient mouth would go on uttering the lines she had prepared. Always, before she appeared in public, these nervous fits assailed her, and more than anything she longed for a kind hand on her brow, a voice saying, 'There, there.'

Jane had ironed the dress Nell had chosen to wear and brought it up, moving on tiptoe. She asked if Nell wanted to wash and had given her a towel that was halfway between a hand towel and a bath towel. Nell said that she might like a drink to steady her nerves — only one — and shortly afterwards, on a tiny little gallery tray, there was a glass of sweet sherry and some oatmeal biscuits. As she changed into the dress, taking her time to fasten the little buttons along the cuffs, the bells from three different churches pealed out, and she said an impromptu prayer and felt dismally alone. As if guessing, her hostess re-entered carrying an electric heater and a patchwork bedcover.

They stood listening to the last peal of the last bell, and Nell thought how Jane was kindness itself in opening her house to a stranger. Not only that, but Jane had gone to the trouble of typing out a list of people at the university whom Nell would meet, adding little dossiers as to their function and what they were like.

'And what do you do apart from teaching?' Nell asked.
'I like to give my time to my family,' Jane said.
'Social life?'
'No, we keep to ourselves,' Jane said, following this with a little smile, a smile with which she punctuated most of her remarks.
Jane took her on a tour of the house then, and Nell saw it all — the three bedrooms besides the guest room with the patchwork quilt, the series of identical shells on the little girl's bureau, the Teddy bear with most of its fur sucked bare, four easy chairs in the living room, and the seven new kittens around the kitchen stove, curled up and as motionless as muffs in a shop window. Jane explained how two kittens were already booked, three would be taken on loan, and the remaining two would stay with the mother and be part of their family. Pinned to the wall in the kitchen was a list of possible Christmas gifts, and when Nell read them she felt some sort of twinge:

Make shirt for Sarah
Grape jelly for Anne
Secondhand book for Josh
Little bottles of bath essence.

The house and its order made such an impression on her that she thought she would like to live in it and be part of its solidity. Then two things happened. A kitten detached itself from the fur mass, stood on its hind legs, and nibbled one of Jane's slippers that was lying there. Then it shadow-boxed, expecting the slipper also to move. Next thing, the hall door opened, someone came in, went through to the parlour, another door was heard to bang, and almost at once Mozart was being played on a fiddle. It was Jane's husband. Jane went to see him, to enquire if he wanted anything, and to tell him that the new guest had come and was very content and had brought a wonderful present — a cut-glass decanter, no less. He seemed not to reply. The fiddle playing went on, and to Nell there was something desperate in it.

Soon after, the two women left for the reading and Jane kept a beautiful silence in the car, allowing Nell to do her deep breathing and memorise her poems. Afterward, they went to a party, and during the party Nell went into the bathroom, watched herself in someone's cracked mirror, and asked herself why it was that everyone was married, or coupled — that everyone had a husband to go home to, a husband to get a drink for, a husband to humour, a husband to deceive — but not she. She wondered if there was some basic attribute missing in her that made her unwifely, or unlovable, and concluded that it must be so. She then had an unbearable longing to be at home in her own house in Ireland, having a solitary drink before bed as she looked out at the River Blackwater.

'What does your husband look like?' she asks of Jane now as they trudge along the road. It is colder than when they set out, and the snow is pelting against their faces. They have to step aside to let a snow plough pass them on the road, and Jane is smiling as she envisages her answer. It is as if she enjoys the prospect of describing her husband, of doing him justice.

'You two girls in trouble?' asks the driver of the snow plough, and they both say that they are simply taking a walk. He shakes his head and seems to think that they are a little mad, then he smiles. His smile reaches them in a haze of snow. They wave him on.

The branches of the birches teeter like swaying children. The icicles are just formed and wet; they look edible and as if they might melt. With her thumbnail Jane flicks open a round locket that hangs from a fine chain about her neck, and there in cameo is a man — gaunt and pensive, very much the type that Nell is drawn towards. At once she feels in herself some premonition of a betrayal.

'He's lovely,' she says, but off-handedly.

' "I don't want you lovely" was what he told me' Jane says.

'Not one of King Arthur's knights,' Nell says, sampling a few flakes of snow.

'It wasn't a romantic thing,' Jane says.

'What was it?' Nell says, nettled.

'It was me very adoring,' Jane says. 'I have a theory it's better that way.'

'I don't believe you,' Nell says, and stands still, causing Jane to stand also, so that she can look into Jane's eyes. They are grey and not particularly fetching, but they are without guile.

'You're prying,' Jane says.

'You're hiding,' Nell says, and they laugh. They are bickering now. they look again at his likeness. The snow has smeared the features, and with her gloved thumb Jane wipes them. Then she snaps the locket closed and drops it down inside her turtleneck sweater — to warm him, she says.

'How did you catch him?' Nell says, putting her arm around Jane and tickling her lightly below her ribs.

'Unfortunatly, I was one of those exceptional women who get pregnant even when they take precautions,' Jane says, shaking her head.

'Was he livid?' Nell says, putting herself in the man's shoes.

'No. He said, "I guess I'll have to marry you, Sarah Jane," and we did.'

It is the 'we' that Nell envies. It has assurance, despite the other woman's non-assertiveness.

'I was married in grey,' Jane says. 'I simply had a prayer book and spring flowers. Dan's mother was so upset about it all that she left during the breakfast. Then we went back to the college, and he read a paper to the students on Mary Shelley.'

'Poor Mary Shelley,' Nell says, feeling a chill all of a sudden, a knife-edged chill that she cannot account for.

'You'd like him,' Jane says, worried by the sudden silence.

'Why would I like him?' Nell says, picturing the face of the man that stared out of the locket. All of a sudden, Nell has a longing not to leave, as planned at six o'clock, for New York, but to stay and meet him.

'Why don't I stay till tomorrow?' she says as casually as she can.

'But that would be wonderful,' Jane says, and without hesitation turns sharply round so that they can hurry home to get the Jerusalem artichokes out of the pit before it has snowed over. She discusses a menu, says Dan will play his favourite pieces for them on the phonograph — adding that he never lets anybody else touch the machine, only himself.

Nell's thought is 'a prison' — a prison such as she had once been in, where the precious objects belonged to the man, and the dusters and brooms belonged to her, the woman.

'He's good to you?' Nell says.

'He's quite good to me,' Jane says.

Men are hunting deer up in the hills, and the noise of the shots volleys across the field with far greater clarity because of the soundlessness created by the snow. Again, on their way back, they pass the snarling dogs and they literally run down a hill and across a stubbled field to take a short cut home. The menu is decided — artichoke soup, roast pork, fried potatoes, and pecan pie. They both profess to be starving.

They pass through a village on the way home and Nell stays behind to buy wine and other treats. She lingers outside the one general store, imagining what it would be like to live in such a place — to be wife, widow, or spinster. She thinks again of her own stone house, the scene of occasional parties and gatherings, when her friends come and she and Biddy, a helper from the village, cook for days; then the aftermath, when they clean up.

The three village churches are white and enveloped in snow; the garage is offering a discount on snow tyres, and an elderly woman is pushing open the door to the general store, bringing back three circulating-library novels. In the shop window are two hand-printed signs:

> We are a family of three sisters looking for a house to rent.
>
> We can afford up to $300.

> LOST: Harvest table, weathered.

She goes inside and buys rashly. Yes, she is curious. Something in Dan's expression makes her tremble with pleasure. Already she has decided on her wardrobe for tonight, and resolves to be timid, in her best sky-blue georgette dress. She buys a gourd filled with sweets for the little girl, and a storm lamp for the little boy.

The children are in the kitchen when she gets back, and how excited they are at receiving these presents. They gabble outrageously about their school lunch, and how gooey it was; then they sing a carol out of harmony; then the little girl admits in a whisper that she loves Nell and gives her a present of a composition she has just written about King Arthur. Nell reads it aloud, and it is about King Arthur looking for a magic harp for his bride, Guinevere. The little boy says it is soppy and his sister whacks him with his new lamp. What can she do to help, Nell asks. Jane says she can do nothing. After the ordeal of the night before, and the fitful sleep because of the boiler going on and off, she must be tired and should nap. Jane tells the children that they must be like little mice and do their homework and not squabble.

There is a harness bell attached to the back door, and it trembles a second before it actually rings and by then he is in. He is like someone out of Nell's childhood — an ascetic man in a long leather coat turned up about the neck, and he wears gauntlet gloves, which he immediately begins to remove. His children run to him; he kisses his wife; and, upon being introduced to Nell, he nods. There is something in that nod that is significant. It is too offhand. Nell sees him look at her with his lids lowered, and she sees him stiffen when his wife says that their guest will stay overnight and then points to the wine. He says, 'Fancy,' as he looks at the labels with approval, and the children ask if they can make butter sauce for the pecan pie.

Nell is having to tell them, the children, the size of her house in Ireland, the kind of ceiling, the cornices, the different wallpapers in the bedrooms, the orchard, the long tree-lined drive, the white gate, the lych gate, the supposed ghost, and everything else pertaining to the place. They say they will visit her when they come to Europe. He does not comment but keeps moving about the kitchen. He looks at the thermometer, pushes the kittens to one side with the toe of his shoe, rakes the stove, and then very slowly begins to open the wine. He smells the corks and very carefully attaches them to the sides of the bottles, using the metallic paper as a cord.

Jane is recalling London — springtime there, a hotel in Bayswater, a trip she had made as a girl with a blind aunt — and remarking to Nell how she saw everything so much more clearly simply by having had to describe it to her aunt. She speaks of the picture galleries, the parks, the little squares, the muffins they were served for breakfast, and the high anthracite-coloured wire meshing around the London Zoo.

'I like being an escort,' she says shyly.

Suddenly Nell has to excuse herself, saying that she must take a last-minute nap, that her eyes feel scorched.

'I can't,' she says later as she lies coiled on her bed, trying to eat back her own tears. All she wants is for the man to come up and nuzzle her and hold her and temporarily squeeze all the solitude out of her. All she wants is a kiss. But that is vicious. She foresees the evening, a replica of other evenings — a look, then ignoring him, then a longer look, a signal, an intuition, a hand maybe, pouring wine, brushing lightly against a wrist, the hair on his knuckles, her chaste cuffs, innocent chatter stoked with something else. She imagines the night — lying awake, creaks, desire fulfilled or unfilled. She sees it all. She bites the bedcover; she makes a face. Every tiny eye muscle is squeezed together. The chill that she felt up on the road is upon her again. She might clench the bedpost, but it is made of brass and is unwelcoming.

'I'm afraid I can't,' she says, bursting into the bathroom where Jane has taken a shower. She knows it is Jane because of the shadow through the glass-panelled door.

'Oh, my dear,' Jane says, pushing the door open and stepping out.

'I just realised it isn't possible,' Nell says, not able to make any excuse except that she has packed and that she must make her plane for New York. Jane says she understands and reaches for a towel to dry herself. Nell begins to help.

'I'm tiny up top,' Jane says, apologising for her little nipples and flat chest. She drags on a thick sweater, slacks, her husband's socks, and then she reaches to a china soap dish and picks up a cluster of hairpins, putting them quickly in her long damp hair.

Dan is in the toolshed, and the two women holler goodbye. The children say, 'No, no, no,' and to make up for this sudden disappointment, Jane and Nell carry them to the car in their slippers and put them under a blanket on the back seat. They will come for the drive. In the car, Jane says that maybe next year, when the attic room is ready, Nell will come back and stay up there and write her poetry. Jane's face is faintly technicolour because of the lights from the dashboard, and her hair is gradually starting to fall down because of the careless way she has put in the hairpins. She looks almost rakish. She says what a shame that Nell has not seen one maple tree in full leaf, to which Nell says yes, that she might come back one day — but she knows that she is just saying this.

Does Jane know, Nell wonders. Does Jane guess? Behind that lovely exterior is Jane a woman who knows all the ways, all the wiles, all the heart's crooked actions?

'Are you jealous, or do you ever have occasion?' Nell asks.

'I have had occasion,' Jane says.

'And what did you do?' Nell asks.

'Well, the first time I made a scene — a bad scene. I threw dishes,' she says, lowering her voice.

'Christ,' Nell says, but is unable to visualise it, is unable to connect the violence with Jane's restraint.

'The second time, I started to teach. I kept busy,' Jane says.

They are driving very slowly, and Nell wonders if, in the back, the children are listening as they pretend to sleep under the blanket. Nell looks out of the window at rows of tombstones covered in snow and evenly spaced. The cemetery is on a hill, and, being just on the outskirts of the town, seems to command it. It seems integral to the town as if the living and the dead are wedded to one another.

'And now?' Nell says.

'I guess Dan and I have had to do some growing up,' Jane says.

'Who's growing up — Daddy?' asks the little girl from under the blanket.

Her mother says, 'Yes, Daddy,' and then adds that his feet are getting bigger.

All four of them laugh.

'He liked you,' Jane says, and gives Nell a little glance.

'I doubt it,' Nell says.

'He sure did,' Jane tells her, convinced.

Nell knows then that Jane has perceived it all and has been willing to let the night and its drama occur. She feels such a tenderness, a current not unlike love, but she does not say a word.

In the airport, they have only minutes to check in the luggage and have Nell's ticket endorsed. The children become exhilarated and pretend to want to place their slippered feet on the conveyor belt so as to get whisked away. The flight is called.

'I think you're very fine,' Nell says at the turnstile by the passenger area.

'Not as fine as you,' Jane says.

Something is waiting to get said. It hangs in the air and Nell recalls the newly formed icicles that they had seen on their walk the day before. More than anything she wants to turn back, to sit in that house, beside the stove, to exchange stories and become a friend of this woman. Politeness drives her forward. Her sleeve catches in the metal pike of the turnstile and Jane picks it out, in the nick of time.

'Clumsy,' Nell says, holding up a cuff with one thread ravelled.

'We're all clumsy,' Jane says.

They exchange a look, and, realising that they are on the

point of either laughing or crying, they say goodbye hurriedly. Ahead of her Nell sees a long slope of linoleum floor and for a minute she's afraid that her legs will not see her safely along it, but they do. Walking down, she smiles and thanks the small voice of instinct that has sent her away without doing the slightest damage to one who met life's vicissitudes with an unquenchable smile.

JOHN MORROW

Beginnings

My first sexual congress — as opposed to that solitary indulgence in the pursuit of which, we're told, we meet a better class of woman — was with a boxmaker's glue-brush. . . . But long before that, in the mid 30s, I had a vivid curtain raiser while on a charabanc trip to the briny with my Aunt Minnie and forty-odd doffers, reelers and winders from our local mill.

It was a long, single-decked, open charabanc with, I think, solid rubber tyres. I, aged five, stood up on the back seat beside Aunt Minnie and waved goodbye to my parents, Father scowling and shaking a last admonitory fist at his sister as we chugged away up the street of mill terraces, the doffers cheering wildly and singing 'Oh I do like to be beside the seaside. . . .'

Father had not liked the idea of his only son, as I then was, being carted off by his sister, whose name he invariably prefaced with the phrase 'that bloody lig'. He'd been on the dole since I'd been born and lately, in despair, had himself been 'Born Again' into a particularly grim set of gospellers; so even if he had been able to afford a trip to the seaside, theologically it was out of the question, the Brethren's last word on the matter being that a man could charabanc to hell just as surely as he who drank, danced, played billiards, hung around chip shops, listened to the wireless or ate ice-cream. The 'bloody lig' (who did all these forbidden things — and more — and who had recently earned Father's further displeasure by being seen to do them — and much more — in the company of a 'dago-dancer' who wore black shirts with *two* rows of white pearl buttons along each collar wing, carried a cut-throat razor in the pocket of his *double-breasted* waistcoat, and had a *shaved* middle-parting) knew all this; which was why I was the only child and, bar the driver, the only male on the charabanc.

En route to the briny Aunt Minnie distributed stout to the girls and lemonade to me. She yelled for the driver to stop a mile beyond the Belfast tram terminus and threatened to turf out two mean sisters unless they paid the final instalment of their fare — which they did. She led the singing (not, I might add, the doleful work songs that I've since heard attributed to mill girls by academic folksingers, but plaintive old melodies such as: 'Fuck the Pope an' no surrender/Bash he's balls agin' the fender . . .' to the tune of 'Dixie'). She stood up on the seat beside me, peroxide perm shattering in the wind, her great bolster of a chest rolling up and down beneath her jumper, and scored a bullseye on the driver's neck with a hard bread bap from the hamper. She was twenty-seven then, a fine looking targe of a woman posed in the middle of a snap taken on Tyrella beach that day, skirt tucked up in the legs of her drawers and me perched on her shoulders, surrounded by her gang of tipsy doffers. . . . (She was still fine looking when the 'dago-dancer' and I lifted her coffin last year — though he, now bald and stooped, complained that the undertaker had made no attempt to erase the snuff stains from her moustache.)

But before we reached Tyrella that day, clipping hedges along the sunlit boreens of County Down, we caught up with the soldiers. . . .

There must have been a full battalion, kilties, company after company strung out in columns of twos with a mounted officer at the head of each, plodding towards Ballykinlar camp in full battle order, tunics of bulls-wool khaki black with sweat. As we approached the rearguard our driver gave a blast on the horn and all the girls began to sing 'Old sodgers never die. . . .' The heads of the rearguard lifted and turned, glengarrys came off and were waved, a ragged cheer rose up. Past the rear company we sped, past the mounted officer who smiled and touched his cap.

I, of course, agog, was cheering and waving and watching the soldiers. The second lot we passed were even more enthusiastic than the rearguard, I noticed, throwing caps in the air and then breaking ranks, straggling out and filling the road in our wake, running, yelling. . . . the officer's horse shying wildly as we roared by. Then I realised that Aunt Minnie and the girls were singing a new song. Looking round, I saw why. Auntie was standing up on the seat, steadying herself with her knees against the folded canvas of the collapsible roof, her jumper rolled up to her armpits, her hands supporting and alternately hefting her bare breasts to the rhythm and content of 'Over my shoulder goes one care/Over my shoulder goes two cares. . . .' Some of the other girls, I saw, were doing likewise, others hoisting their skirts. The road behind was a solid mass of cheering soldiers; caps flew; rifles were brandished; horses reared and whinnied. One small jock, rifle, pack and cap discarded, ran almost apace with us for some distance, gazing up at Auntie's bobbing beauties with an expression as set and tense as any Olympic pole-vaulter, the front of his kilt reefed up over an enormous erection. . . until a sergeant brought him down with a flying tackle and lay on him.

This last cameo as we sped past the routed column caused further widening in the rift between Aunt Minnie and Father at the end of our glorious day by the sea . . . . 'an' we had ice-cream an' chips an' cuckles,' I listed breathlessly (Father frowned) . . . . 'An' paddled an' this wee kiltie tried to catch Aunt Minnie's diddies,' (Father blew up).

Now I'm not suggesting that with this incident all was revealed to me at the age of five; on the contrary, it left me with the same mistaken impression Steinbeck speculates a visiting Martian might get from viewing Coca Cola adverts — 'that the seat of human procreation is in the mammary glands' — (a misconception put right for me about half-way between the charabanc ride and the glue-brush by a she-cousin who began by showing me how, when wrestling, instead of punching her in the stomach I could more readily incapacitate her by tickling further down). Yet the memory of Auntie's big brown nipples performing in the sunlight, and that wee jock's standing ovation, does loom out from the mire of half-truths, hearsay and doubtful fact one accumulates during an up-the-entry sex education.

In 1944, aged thirteen, I started work as a part-timer in a cardboard box factory, 'spoken for' by a lady boxmaker who Endeavoured For Christ's Sake with my Mother. For three hours daily after school (3/6 per week) I was to keep the place tidy, maintain a supply of materials to the workers and do local deliveries with a two-wheeled hand-cart, roped between the shafts like a donkey (sounds wildly Dickensian, but it's the God's truth — on many a winter's day, skidding like mad on a black icy incline, I'd have changed places with any warm, dry little chimney sweep).

Boxmakers considered themselves a cut above weavers, doffers, stitchers and the like; and indeed most of the twenty or so ladies who worked in pairs on either side of the steaming glue-wells were of the settled type, wives and mothers in early middle age, many, like Mrs. Poots, Mother's friend, 'Saved'. They sang hymns rather than 'Juanita' or 'Roll me over in the clover' and passed the time challenging one another on Biblical text rather than 'telling' pictures or swapping dirty yarns. But there were others in the place, a few unskilled girls who worked the various machines for preparing the cardboard, and it was one of these, the clart on the guillotine, who sent me to my first humiliation.

Father, now back to shipyard, football terrace and boozer, had warned me about 'cod-ons' — the apprentice sent traipsing from shed to shed in search of 'the rubber-headed hammer' or 'a bucket of blue steam'; but Father had never worked with women. . . . So when the guillotine wench — a dark, pseudo-shy little thing who arrived and departed each day by jeep or staff car — gave me a threepenny bit and sent me to the chemists for 'a two-dee tin of two-lip salve', I went all in innocence.

Even now I cringe inwardly on recalling the stunned expression on the face of the chemist's female assistant and the outbreak of snorts and titters from customers, also female, who stood around awaiting prescriptions. 'We have none,' says the bitch, 'try Mr. Coll's down the street.' An uproar of shrieks and guffaws followed me through the door; but I, still unaware, went down to Mr. Coll's.

Luckily Mr. Coll himself was serving and I was the only customer. He was old and gruff. 'You're from the box-makers,' he growled after I'd stated my business. 'Which one of them sent you?'

I told him.

'Huh! The squaw . . . I might have known,' he said, and, leaning over the high, glass counter, he went on: 'Now what I want you to do is go straight back and tell her . . . .'

So I went back to the machine room and told the guillotine girl, standing expectantly in a circle of her workmates, all bursting with suppressed giggles: 'Mr. Coll says he's only got pint tins of the stuff you want. But he says that as a pint would be no good to you, if you'll send over the biggest bucket you can find. . . .' That's as far as I got, for all within earshot screamed with delight — all, that is, except the squaw herself. And barely a week later, when I, poor gomeral, still couldn't fathom what I'd done to merit the knowing smirks and, to me, incomprehensible innuendo directed at me since the 'two-lip salve' incident, she had her revenge with the glue-brush.

When it happened I was engaged in supplying the box-makers with stacks of prepared cardboard, a task onerous on green muscles, for I had to hump them two-handed the length of the workroom from the machines to the benches. The ladies were going into the second verse of 'Bringing In The Sheaves', I remember, as I tottered under my fourth or fifth load to Mrs. Poots' place. The bench was more than my-waist-high, and just as I was hoisting my burden up to slide it into a handy position beside her glue-well, homely bespectacled Mrs. Poots, Mother's comrade in Christian Endeavour, trilled 'Working for the Master . . .' and ripped open my fly! (I should say 'spare', for in those days zips were a laughable Yankee eccentricity, just as underpants were considered, at least in our strata of Prod poverty, somehow immoral.) So you'll see that, my first line of defence gone, all I had was a long shirt-tail — and that soon, as they say, 'went up like a windybline'.

I dropped the cardboard. A cheer, a rush of feet, and I was grabbed from behind by many muscular arms lifted, and spreadeagled on Mrs. Poots' bench alongside her stinking glue-well. A chant ringing in my ears — 'Sticky Dicky, Sticky Dicky' — my long shirt-tail up at my chin, the grinning squaw kneeling on the bench beside me, brandishing a steaming, dripping glue-brush . . . . the chant changing to 'Rosebud, Rosebud' (Fagan, apparently, had retired to deep cover) . . . . a warm sensation as the squaw applied her brush liberally, and the tremulous giggling of Mrs. Poots, who lay across my right arm murmuring, over and over: 'Ah God forgive us, God forgive us.'

Released, I upped and ran the whole cut home with the glue quickly hardening around my jewels in the cold air. Luckily there was no one in the house at that time of day and with hot water and scrubbing brush I managed to get most of it off before it reached a prep and surgery state of solidity.

I swore to myself that I'd never set foot in the kip again; I hatched all sorts of heinous revenge plots; but I told no one outside what had happened — except my best friend at school the next day. He saw it as having given me *carte blanche* to enact all *his* sexual fantasies on every female in the factory, one by one. He grew very excited as he sketched his scenario of depravity (all of which, I learned later, he'd cribbed from an album of photographs his Da had looted from a dead Turk in the Dardanelles) and stated that if I didn't return to the job he'd apply for it.

Whatever drove me to clock-in the following afternoon — the thought of my 3/6 going into his pocket, sexual curiosity, the prospect of Father's wrath — I can't recall; but I do recall the cheer that went up when I entered the workroom, and the song with which the hussies round the machines greeted me — an early, dirty version of 'I've got a luvly bunch of coconuts . . .' The squaw smiled slyly and mouthed 'Rosebud' at me. A sheepish Mrs. Poots gave me a wine gum.

From then until I left school and started full-time in the shipyard I went unmolested. Two weeks before I departed, the squaw did, having been driven by circumstances (four months gone, five to go) to make her choice from amongst the occupying forces. As is the tradition, we all contributed to a wedding present; and on the day she left to accompany her full-blooded Navajo sergeant to his ranch in the far west — one of the first, and most advanced, G.I. brides — she was submitted to another bit of tradition. This involved her being manhandled into roughly the same position on the bench as I had been, and, in place of the brush, the application of a do-it-yourself dildo in hardened glue, lovingly moulded beforehand (that Mrs. Poots!). As a mark of my maturity, I like to think, I was allowed to hold a leg and perform some subsidiary, dexterous skirmishing on my own part; altogether a final eye-opener, anatomically speaking.

VAL MULKERNS

Humanae Vitae

After rain, the washed blue sky glittered above the choppy sea, but the East wind was cold. 'See', the man in the sheepskin coat said smugly, 'I brought that bit of sun with me.' Cliches were so seldom used as opening gambits that the wife glanced sharply at him before smiling.

'I could show you the Mass rock I wrote to you about,' she said. 'It's better in the very late evening, just before sunset, but it may be raining by then.'

'Almost certainly. So show me. Not more than seven miles there and back?'

'It's much less, honestly. Michael and I did it a few nights ago before his bedtime. Mrs. O'Friel puts the others to bed for me whenever I want to go out.'

'Nice Mrs. O'Friel. I liked her immediately.'

The wife glanced up, surprised and pleased, as she tried to measure her quick strides to his slow ones over the rocky fields behind the house. 'She was delighted when she heard you were coming up for the last week—you wouldn't believe the fuss there was the last few days. She wanted to know would I like to change my room when the Flynns went because the wardrobe was bigger and you could see that headland from the window—it's called Reenamara, by the way. Look, over there.'

'Oh, yes.'

'It's where you get the best lobsters. Wee Tommy fishes them out from under the rocks with a stick which has a hook on the end of it.'

'You've seen this?'

'Yes. The boys and I went on a lobster hunt with the O'Friels last week. The Flynns and some others came too. You must come with us one day next week.'

'Who's Wee Tommy while he's at home or abroad?'

'He's Mr. O'Friel. But nobody calls him anything but Wee Tommy—he's so small that his son Hugh could carry him for seven miles on his back without even noticing the difference.'

'Hugh does this often?'

'Don't be silly!' The wife, giggling, skipped ahead at last at her own pace, jumping from one reedy tussock of grass to another over the marshy pale green patches which at dusk could be treacherous. She went on skipping until she reached the first grey slabs of rock, and then she sat down and lifted her face to the sun, eyes closed, leaning back on the palms of her hands, smiling. Just before the man reached her, he became aware that she was watching his slow progress through smiling slitted eyes, and he stumbled on one of the tussocks, misjudged the jump to the next one, and ended up cursing on the pale boggy moss, up to the tops of his socks in water. Her laugh died quickly when she saw his angry face, but he was beside her, laughing at himself, in a few moments, her shoulders gripped in his hands, his rough five o'clock chin rasping her forehead until she called for mercy.

'This was never my country,' he intoned, 'I was not born nor bred nor reared here and it will not have me alive nor dead. But it may well be the end of me!'

She laughed and went on laughing. 'Take off your socks,' she said, 'and I'll hang them out of my belt to dry in the wind.' She was wearing a jersey and blue jeans with a sort of leather scout's belt which had loops made for carrying various objects.

'They'll dry just as easily on me, and probably much quicker,' the man said.

'Wee Tommy wouldn't agree with you about ignoring wet feet. You know what he does? Before he steps out into the shallow pools at low tide he takes off his socks and puts them in his pocket. Then he rolls up his trouser legs and puts his boots back on again.'

'You mean Wellingtons?'

'I mean ordinary black leather boots. And he steps out

into the pools in these so that they're sopping wet by the time he's finished.'

'Don't tell me. Then he takes them off and puts on his dry socks. Then he puts the boots back on, and before he's gone ten paces his socks are as wet as the boots! He could save himself a lot of trouble by just stepping out in the first place.'

'You're wrong. The dry socks *stay* dry, he says, and the boots have dried out by the time he gets home.'

'Obstinate self-deceiving peasants!' the man exploded, but good-humouredly, and he took her hand to pull her to her feet. He kept the hand in a tight warming grip as they walked along, as easily as though on a road because here the rocks were in flat slab formations. Small pink flowers like candytuft grew in the crevices and bent double in the sea wind. The sea itself had temporarily disappeared, though they could hear it roaring in the caves underneath.

'How was it at home when you left this morning?' the wife asked.

'All right. Mrs. Cuffe said to tell you that after three weeks the dogs are so lonely for you that they've begun to be friendly with *her,* and they even eat the tinned stuff occasionally.'

'Poor dogs. What about you?'

'I'll tell you later how I am,' he grinned, and squeezed her hand until it hurt. 'Oh, by the way, I've been messing with your sun place and you may even like it.'

'Please, what have you done?'

'You just wait and see. And I let the grandchildren staying next door strip the raspberries, and then I did over the paths with sodium chlorate. Oh, and Mrs. Cuffe took home some windfalls to make jelly.'

'Did Joan ask you over to a meal as she said?'

'She did, but I managed to get out of it.'

'Micheal!'

'I was perfectly tactful, don't worry.'

'Wait till you taste a lobster that's only been out of the tide for half an hour! After weeks of basic eating, you're going to enjoy this week, I can tell you. We'll probably go out with Wee Tommy again—let's see, this is Saturday. Tuesday the tide should be right again for lobsters. I bet he'll be going on Tuesday and we can all go with him.'

'You've forgotten I don't particularly like the beasts.'

'Wait till you taste one that's been crawling around the kitchen floor until the moment it's put into the boiling water!'

Cormorants screamed around their heads as they climbed the last barbed wire fence stubbornly fixed to the bare rock. 'Who,' the man wanted to know, 'but these land-hungry famine relics would bother to fix a boundary to such barrenness? Who would be likely to dispute ownership with them except these gulls?'

'If it were mine, I'd do exactly the same,' the wife said. 'Look, this is the last stretch. Do you see where the rocks form a sort of semi-circle, like half a Greek stage? Well, that's Carraig-an-Aifrinn. It's just at the innermost point.'

'Let's just say we've seen it, then. Look at those clouds making straight for us.' Rain clouds had clotted together beyond the next headland and were blowing lightly as the white cumulus across the dwindling stretch of blue sky. He held her shoulders from behind and tightened her backwards against his ribs. Then with one finger he lifted her chin up so that she had to see the clouds.

'It will just about catch us, if it does rain, when we've arrived at the rock and there we have shelter,' she said.

She broke away as she had done earlier and ran, beckoning him, across the bright granite, her ridged shoes gripping fast even when she leaped across the now frequent gashes in the rockface through which the sea spumed below. The man shrugged and buttoned his sheepskin higher, then followed in the same direction though not in her footsteps. When he chose he could stride faster than she, and this he did, avoiding most of the jumps by taking the long way around them, and arriving at the fanlike circle of rocks only a little after she did and only a little more breathless.

'See if you can find it,' she invited, elbows leaning on a table of rock that was not a dolmen but looked very similar. The man fancied he could feel the stone cold against her breasts; she never could be taught to wear enough clothes underneath.

'You're irreverently leaning on it, of course.'

'Wrong. I wouldn't.' She was smiling.

The man shrugged and raised his collar against the first blown drops of rain. Then he quickly stepped around her side of the rock, pulled a blue scarf out of her pocket and tied it under her chin.

'What's wrong with you is you are not safe to let out,' he said, but now he was smiling. 'Look, while you propose this cute game of hide and seek those dirty black clouds are about to disgorge their whole load on top of us.'

Still smiling, the wife shook off her scarf and beckoned him. He followed, into the broken circle of rocks, some of which dripped as though the sea had somehow forced entry from below and bled through them. But when she stopped abruptly and stepped behind a mound of small rocks—like the cairn on a mountain summit—it was suddenly dry, and the limestone altar stone was unmistakable although much smaller than the exposed table he had seen at first. Up behind it the rock face with it's savage fissures soared a hundred feet into the air so that one thought of a Gothic cathedral until one came face to face with the sky, with the one triangle of blue that remained.

'Look!' the wife said, and emptied a small heap of coins into his hand. He had not noticed that the altar was littered with these, sixpenny pieces and shillings of worn silver, halfpence and pence and (surely?) about seven half-sovereigns. These were what she had put into his hand and he turned them over curiously.

'Can't understand why somebody hasn't knocked these off,' he said, 'How did they escape?'

'Who *would* take them?—it's a holy place.'

When he turned from replacing the gold coins she was on her knees, fair head bent, but she got up almost immediately when a rainy bitter gust of wind practically took their breath away.

'I know where to go,' she said, and he followed her a few yards away into a shallow cave, invisible from where they had been standing. Inside, it was dry, with a floor of small pebbles and the shells of sea-snails which, some time, might have been carried there by high tides. Pleased, he took off his sheepskin and spread it inside out on the pebbles. Suddenly he was reminded of their courtship. When she plumped down, giggling at the perfection of the shelter she had provided, he was instantly beside her, bulky and warm, breathing very fast, amorous urgently as was his way, joking about the ghosts of decent Mass-going peasants that were this very minute about to be startled.

The wife's immediate response was abruptly checked and she broke from him to sit back uncertainly on her heels, cold hands cupping her knees. She saw the astonishment in his eyes, and when she spoke her voice did not quite register the levity she had intended. 'Perhaps we'd better make a date for same time, same place on Monday. It *ought* to have been O.K. today, but I was late, and it isn't. Unless you want twins or something by this time next year.'

'Oh God no!' At home he'd even checked the marked calendar on the inside of his wardrobe. But this was a calendar you could never quite rely on. Yet he had relied on it for the whole length of that journey. Two hundred miles had never seemed so short.

'You're not any sorrier than I am,' she complained, turning away to dig into the small pebbles with her fingers.

'Sorry, yes, but you'll go on waiting for a celibate churchman in Mother Rome to change his mind again, won't you? How long is it going to take him to realise that though the Church may have spoken, the people of God have long since passed out of earshot?'

'I haven't. And he isn't just a celibate churchman. He's the Pope.'

'You haven't. And he's the Pope. And he has the right to

tell you when *your* marriage vows made before God may be honoured and when not?'

'Yes, he has the right,' the wife said, on the note of stubborn finality that goes with old arguments. She was still playing with a handful of the small pebbles as he got angrily to his feet and stamped over to the mouth of the cave. For several minutes he stared out into the driving rain. Once she thought he was going to make off into it, but he came back shaking himself like a dog, with something like calm restored to his face.

'Don't imagine I came all the way up here to go into all *that* again,' he said.

'Monday's not really so far away,' the wife placated, and he opened his mouth to reply but quickly changed his mind.

He went onto another tack. 'Trouble with you is you never see beyond these desolate rainy wastes,' he said. 'Look at us! Huddled on a summer's day in a damp cave on the edge of the Atlantic with the rain and the furious sea thundering all around us and not even sex to keep us warm, and you think we should be happy.'

'I am, but I'd be happier if it was Monday. And the floor of the cave is bone dry—feel.'

'Out there are sun and civilisations the sun nurtured—do you think the culture of Greece could have happened at all in a climate like this?'

'You can hardly call this place uncivilised all the same. Think of the imagination that saw this as the perfect natural place of worship that it is—and closely hidden as it had to be.'

'Think of them,' the man mused, 'straggling in their famine tatters across the rocks with the rain beating down on them, spouting their barbaric language at one another, with their fists clenched tight over the halfpence they wouldn't have been welcomed without.'

'Not true. The celebrant of a Penal Mass risked death every time he celebrated it, remember. If he had to live on the halfpence of the poor, that was hardly his fault. They gave freely.'

'What puzzles me is why they continued to give after the whole show was over. What's the meaning of those coins, most of which are no more than a century old? Don't tell *me* any priest couldn't bear to take the pence of the poor.'

'It puzzles me too. I think maybe the money was offered up perhaps in gratitude for Emancipation or something.'

'Offered to God? Money? You see, our own peculiar form of superstitious lunacy! Like the Thanksgiving notices you see only in Irish newspapers. "Grateful thanks to St. Anthony for great favour received." Is the Irish Clarion delivered by carrier pigeon to the celestial gates at ten o'clock sharp every morning? Or does St. Anthony come down for a free read of the files every so often to find out who the lousers are who haven't even bothered to thank him?'

Now the wife was laughing too, but she stopped soon. 'I'm taking you to meet Páid Eoin tonight in O'Donnell's pub,' she said, jumping up suddenly. 'He'll tell you more than I can about this place—which, by the way, is haunted.'

'We are *not* going to listen to a *sean duine liath* giving out old guff over his booze tonight?'

'Of course we are. It's great fun, and I promise you'll like him. Aren't you curious to know who haunts Carraig-an-Aifrinn? That I do know.'

'It's haunted by a pair of drunken tailors who dropped three halfpence through a slit in the rock on their way to Mass one rainy morning after Samhain. They've never quite given up hope of finding the money. So every night when the moon is full——'

'Keep quiet and listen. Two men and a pregnant woman came over in a currach from the island one Sunday morning. Can you imagine landing a currach on those rocks down there even in good weather? It seems the woman's brother was capable of handling a currach anywhere along this coast and her husband was nearly as good. But a storm blew up suddenly—it was October—and they were drowned like the Armada sailors trying to land. They were seen in broad daylight on the edge of the crowd at Mass a short time afterwards and they still haunt these rocks.'

'Very nice. Pregnant with her seventeenth child no doubt. Now come on before we hear them caterwauling—God knows it's dark enough though the rain seems to have stopped.' He pulled her to her feet, kissed her lightly by way of peace offering and buttoned himself back into his sheepskin. They strolled, arm in arm, back along the wet roads of rock.

'Look' said the wife, 'I wouldn't doubt him. Will you look at Micheal coming to find us?'

The ten-year-old in an Aran gansey was bounding like a goat towards them over the rocks, whooping a war-cry in case they hadn't seen him. He arrived breathless but articulate. 'The others are furious, Daddy, that you got away without them. I guessed where Mummy had taken you so I thought—thought I'd just meet you on the way back.' He grinned, his freckled face sheepish.

'Well timed, Michael,' the father applauded.

'Know what?' the boy said in his mother's ear, 'Hugh's just brought in a huge salmon for Daddy's supper.'

'You don't mean it?'

'Sure. And Daddy, Hugh says will you come out fishing with us in the boat on Monday?'

'I couldn't bear the cold in my aged bones.'

'But Daddy, he has oilskins for us, and I was too hot, out in the boat last week—even in the rain.'

'Look at those other scoundrels coming out after you,' the man said abruptly, and when they waved the four remote figures in blue shorts scrambled like crabs over the rocks, uttering faint aggrieved shouts as they came.

Up in the ghost village of Kilcreeshla there were hardly any lights. The green road that led to another village (now totally deserted) was invisible to all but those who knew it was there. Kilcreeshla itself had only four schoolgoing children and as many as forty old people, so most of the stone cottages which were not abandoned were asleep early and showed no lights. Two houses built together at right angles to the road were bright, however, and bicycles leaned against the gable end. A few visitors' cars were parked together in the open flagged yard where hens picked during the day time. When the door opened, a blast of warm talk and firelight escaped into the night air, but the man and woman who weaving latched the door at once behind them, and only the wheeze of an old melodeon could be heard following them down the rocky overgrown road.

'We left before the fun really started,' the wife protested, 'You've no idea how good it gets later. Peadar hadn't even warmed up for his step dance and Páid Eoin was only on his second pint. He never begins yarning until he's well into his third one.'

'Then we *did* leave at the right time,' the man grinned. 'You *know* I can't stand these whiskery ancients with their Old Moore's wisdom. You can have them all to yourself tomorrow night,' he finished on a coaxing note, and then realised he'd said more than he intended at this juncture.

'You mean you won't come out tomorrow night?'

'I mean I won't be here tomorrow night,' he said gently, an arm tightened about her waist as they walked down the hill to the crossroads. 'I only came up to say, so to speak, that I couldn't come. I only knew I couldn't yesterday, and you were all expecting me and I thought it was better——'

'Why?'

'O'Kelly isn't satisfied with the price. I must be in town before ten on Monday morning to see if I can push the deal through. It's possible that it may take several days. I must set off from here soon after lunch tomorrow.'

'I mean why did you come just to say you weren't coming? That was stupid. All those preparations the O'Friels were making——'

'Stuff the O'Friels. I came to see you. Two hundred miles up here and the same back tomorrow, just to see you.

I didn't like to write or telegraph.'

'It would have been better.'

'Look, you're not crying, are you?'

'I'm *not* crying. But you can tell Mrs. O'Friel yourself—I'm not going to. I know you mentioned about this O'Kelly thing in the last letter, but I didn't think it was so important. Is it a woman?'

'Sheila, you're crazy. What the hell would I want with a woman? I've got one.'

'If it is a woman, you can take her to beautiful Greece with you, for all I care. No, let me go. I'm going back to the pub, and I'll walk back later with Wee Tommy as I do every other night. Grass widowhood's nothing new to me, remember.'

'Wee Tommy will be as drunk as a lord and will probably get sick all over your shoes.'

'I'll risk that.'

'I'm sorry. Won't you believe that I'm *sorry?"*

'I believe you. Think of me on Monday night in town and I'll do you the same favour here. Good night. You'll be asleep by the time I get back.' Her tone made it clear that this was as she wanted it to be.

Then, more quickly than he had anticipated, she twisted away from him and ran back towards the pub. He followed her slowly for a few steps, and then stopped when the blast of light and sound came again as she lifted the latch. The door closed at once, and he stood for several minutes in the darkness on the stony path, staring at the place where the light had been, listening to the faint wheeze of the old melodeon. Then he walked back in the direction of the crossroads, cursing softly in the silence that was broken now and again by the unseen incoming tide.

WILLIAM TREVOR

An Evening with John Joe Dempsey

In Keogh's one evening Mr Lynch talked about the Piccadilly tarts, and John Joe Dempsey on his fifteenth birthday closed his eyes and travelled into a world he did not know. 'Big and little,' said Mr Lynch, 'winking their eyes at you and enticing you up to them. Wetting their lips.' said Mr Lynch, 'with the ends of their tongues.'

John Joe Dempsey had walked through the small town that darkening autumn evening, from the far end of North Street where he and his mother lived, past the cement building that was the Coliseum Cinema, past Kelly's Atlantic Hotel and a number of shops that were now closed for the day. 'Go to Keogh's like a good boy,' his mother had requested, for as well as refreshments and stimulants Keogh's public house sold a variety of groceries: it was for a pound of rashers that Mrs Dempsey had sent her son.

'Who is there?' Mr Lynch had called out from the licensed area of the premises, hearing John Joe rapping with a coin to draw attention to his presence. A wooden partition with panes of glass in the top half of it rose to a height of eight feet between the grocery and the bar. 'I'm here for rashers,' John Joe explained through the pebbly glass. 'Isn't it a stormy evening, Mr Lynch? I'm fifteen today, Mr Lynch.'

There was a silence before a door in the partition opened and Mr Lynch appeared. 'Fifteen?' he said. 'Step in here, boy, and have a bottle of stout.'

John Joe protested that he was too young to drink a bottle of stout and then said that his mother required the rashers immediately. 'Mrs Keogh's gone out to Confession,' Mr Lynch said. 'I'm in charge till her ladyship returns.'

John Joe, knowing that Mr Lynch would not be prepared to set the bacon machine in action, stepped into the bar to await the return of Mrs Keogh, and Mr Lynch darted behind the counter for two bottles of stout. Having opened and poured them, he began about the Piccadilly tarts.

'You've got to an age,' Mr Lynch said, 'when you would have to be advised. Did you ever think in terms of emigration to Britain?'

'I did not, Mr Lynch.'

'I would say you were right to leave it alone, John Joe. Is that the first bottle of stout you ever had?'

'It is, Mr Lynch.'

'A bottle of stout is an acquired taste. You have to have had a dozen bottles or maybe more before you do get an urge for it. With the other matter it's different,'

Mr. Lynch, now a large, fresh-faced man of fifty-five who was never seen without a brown hat on his head, had fought for the British Army during the Second World War, which was why one day in 1947 he had found himself, with companions, in Piccadilly Circus. As he listened, John Joe recalled that he'd heard boys at the Christian Brothers' referring to some special story that Mr. Lynch confidentially told to those whom he believed would benefit from it. He had heard boys sniggering over this story, but he had never sought to discover its content, not knowing it had to do with Piccadilly tarts.

'There was a fellow by the name of Baker,' said Mr. Lynch, 'who'd been telling us that he know the ropes. Baker was a London man. He knew the places, he was saying, where he could find the glory girls, but when it came to the point of the matter, John Joe, we hardly needed a guide.'

Because, explained Mr. Lynch, the tarts were

everywhere. They stood in the doorways of shops showing off the stature of their legs. Some would speak to you, Mr. Lynch said, addressing you fondly and stating their availability. Some had their bosoms cocked out so that maybe they'd strike a passing soldier and entice him away from his companions. 'I'm telling you this, John Joe, on account of your daddy being dead. Are you fancying that stout?'

John Joe nodded his head. Thirteen years ago his father had fallen to his death from a scaffold, having been by trade a builder. John Joe could not remember him, although he knew what he had looked like from a photograph that was always on view on the kitchen dresser. He had often wondered what it would be like to have that bulky man about the house, and more often still he listened to his mother talking about him. But John Joe didn't think about his father now, in spite of Mr. Lynch's reference to him: keen to hear more about the women of Piccadilly, he asked what had happened when Mr. Lynch and his companions finished examining them in the doorways.

'I saw terrible things in Belgium,' replied Mr. Lynch meditatively. 'I saw a Belgian woman held down on the floor while four men satisfied themselves on her. No woman could be the same after that. Combat brings out the brute in a man.'

'Isn't it shocking what they'd do, Mr. Lynch? Wouldn't it make you sick?'

'If your daddy was alive today, he would be telling you a thing or two in order to prepare you for your manhood and the temptations in another country. Your mother wouldn't know how to tackle a matter like that, nor would Father Ryan, nor the Christian Brothers. Your daddy might have sat you down in this bar and given you your first bottle of stout. He might have told you about the facts of life.'

'Did one of the glory girls entice yourself, Mr. Lynch?'

'Listen to me, John Joe.' Mr. Lynch regarded his companion through small blue eyes, both of which were slightly bloodshot. He lit a cigarette and drew on it before continuing. Then he said: 'Baker had the soldiers worked up with his talk of the glory girls taking off their togs. He used to describe the motion of their haunches. He used to lie there at night in the dug-out describing the private areas of the women's bodies. When the time came we went out with Baker and Baker went up to the third one he saw and said could the six of us make arrangements with her. He was keen to strike a bargain because we had only limited means on account of having remained in a public house for four hours. Myself included, we were in an intoxicated condition.'

'What happened, Mr. Lynch?'

'I would not have agreed to an arrangment like that if it hadn't been for drink. I was a virgin boy, John Joe. Like yourself.'

'I'm that way, certainly, Mr. Lynch.'

'We marched in behind the glory girl, down a side-street. "Bedad, you're fine men," she said. We had bottles of beer in our pockets. "We'll drink that first," she said, "before we get down to business." '

John Joe laughed. He lifted the glass of stout to his lips and took a mouthful in a nonchalant manner, as though he'd been drinking stout for half a lifetime and couldn't do without it.

'Aren't you the hard man, Mr. Lynch!' he said.

'You've got the wrong end of the stick,' replied Mr. Lynch sharply. 'What happened was, I had a vision on the street. Amn't I saying to you those girls are no good to any man? I had a vision of the Virgin when we were walking along.'

'How d'you mean, Mr. Lynch?"

'There was a little statue of the Holy Mother in my bedroom at home, a little special one my mother gave me at the occasión of my First Communion. It came into my mind, John Joe, when the six of us were with the glory girl. As soon as the glory girl said we'd drink the beer before we got down to business I saw the statue of the Holy Mother, as clear as if it was in front of me.'

John Joe, who had been anticipating an account of the soldiers' pleasuring, displayed disappointment. Mr. Lynch shook his head at him.

'I was telling you a moral story,' he said reprovingly. 'The facts of life is one thing, John Joe, but keep away from dirty women.'

John Joe was a slight youth, pale of visage, as his father had been, and with large, awkward hands that bulged in his trouser pockets. He had no friends at the Christian Brothers' School he attended, being regarded there, because of his private nature and lack of interest in either scholastic or sporting matters, as something of an oddity — an opinion that was strengthened by his association with an old, simple-minded dwarf called Quigley, with whom he was regularly to be seen collecting minnows in a jam-jar or walking along the country roads. In class at the Christian Brothers' John Joe would drift into a meditative state and could not easily be reached. 'Where've you gone, boy?' Brother Leahy would whisper, standing above him. His fingers would reach out for a twist of John Joe's scalp, and John Joe would rise from the ground with the Brother's thumb and forefinger tightening the short hairs of his neck, yet seeming not to feel the pain. It was only when the other hand of Brother Leahy gripped one of his ears that he would return to the classroom with a cry of anguish, and the boys and Brother Leahy would laugh. 'What'll we make of you?' Brother Leahy would murmur, returning to the blackboard while John Joe rubbed his head and his ear.

'There is many a time in the years afterwards,' said Mr. Lynch ponderously, 'when I have gone through in my mind that moment in my life. I was tempted in bad company: I was two minutes off damnation.'

'I see what you mean, Mr. Lynch.'

'When I came back to West Cork my mother asked me was I all right. Well, I was, I said. "I had a bad dream about you," my mother said. "I had a dream one night your legs were on fire." She looked at my legs, John Joe, and to tell you the truth of it she made me slip down by britches. "There's no harm there," she said. 'Twas only afterwards I worked it out: she had that dream in the very minute I was standing on the street seeing the vision in my brain. What my mother dreamed, John Joe, was that I was licked by the flames of Hell. She was warned that time, and from her dream she sent out a message that I was to receive a visit from the little statue. I'm an older man now, John Joe, but that's an account I tell to every boy in this town that hasn't got a father. That little story is an introduction to life and manhood. Did you enjoy the stout?'

'The stout's great stuff, Mr. Lynch.'

'No drink you can take, John Joe, will injure you the way a dirty woman would. You might go to twenty million Confessions and you wouldn't relieve your heart and soul of a dirty woman. I didn't marry myself, out of shame for the memory of listening to Baker making that bargain. Will we have another bottle?'

John Joe, wishing to hear in further detail the bargain that Baker had made, said he could do with another drop. Mr. Lynch directed him to a crate, behind the counter, 'You're acquiring the taste', he said.

John Joe opened and poured the bottles. Mr. Lynch offered him a cigarette, which he accepted. In the Coliseum Cinema he had seen Piccadilly Circus, and in one particular film there had been Piccadilly tarts, just as Mr. Lynch described, loitering in doorways provocatively. As always, coming out of the Coliseum, it had been a a little strange to find himself again among small shops that sold clothes and hardware and meat, among vegetable shops and tiny confectioners' and tobacconists' and public houses. For a few minutes after the Coliseum's programme was over the three streets of the town were busy with people going home, walking or riding on bicycles, or driving cars to distant farms, or going towards the chip-shop. When he was alone, John Joe usually leaned against the window of a shop to watch the activity before returning home himself; when his mother accompanied him to the pictures they naturally went home at once, his mother chatting on about the film they'd seen.

'The simple thing is, John Joe, keep a certain type of thought out of your mind.'

'Thought, Mr. Lynch?'

'Of a certain order.'

'Ah, yes. Ah, definitely, Mr. Lynch. A young fellow has no time for that class of thing.'

'Live a healthy life.'

'That's what I'm saying, Mr. Lynch.'

'If I hadn't had a certain type of thought I wouldn't have found myself on the street that night. It was Baker who called them the glory girls. It's a peculiar way of referring to the sort they are.'

'Excuse me, Mr. Lynch, but what kind of an age would they be?'

'They were all ages, boy. There were nippers and a few more of them had wrinkles on the flesh of their faces. There were some who must have weighed fourteen stone and others you could put in your pocket.'

'And was the one Baker made the bargain with a big one or a little one?'

'She was medium sized, boy.'

'And had she black hair, Mr. Lynch?'

'As black as your boot. She had a hat on her head that was a disgrace to the nation, and black gloves on her hands. She was carrying a little umbrella.'

'And, Mr. Lynch, when your comrades met up with you again, did they tell you a thing at all?'

Mr. Lynch lifted the glass to his lips. He filled his mouth with stout and savoured the liquid before allowing it to pass into his stomach. He turned his small eyes on the youth and regarded him in silence.

'You have pimples on your chin,' said Mr. Lynch in the end. 'I hope you're living a clean life, now.'

'A healthy life, Mr. Lynch.'

'It is a question your daddy would ask you. You know

what I mean? There's some lads can't leave it alone.'

'They go mad in the end, Mr. Lynch.'

'There was fellows in the British Army that couldn't leave it alone.'

'They're a heathen crowd, Mr. Lynch. Isn't there terrible reports in the British papers?'

'The body is God-given. There's no need to abuse it.'

'I've never done that thing, Mr. Lynch.'

'I couldn't repeat' said Mr. Lynch, 'what the glory girl said when I walked away.'

John Joe, whose classroom meditations led him towards the naked bodies of women whom he had seen only clothed and whose conversations with the town's idiot, Quigley, were of an obscene nature, said it was understandable that Mr. Lynch could not repeat what the girl had said to him. A girl like that, he added, wasn't fit to be encountered by a decent man.

'Go behind the counter,' said Mr. Lynch, 'and lift out two more bottles.'

John Joe walked to the crate of stout bottles. 'I looked in at a window one time,' Quigley had said to him, 'and I saw Mrs. Nugent resisting her husband. Nugent took no notice of her at all; he had the clothes from her body like you'd shell a pod of peas.'

'I don't think Baker lived,' said Mr. Lynch. 'He'd be dead of disease.'

'I feel sick to think of Baker, Mr. Lynch.'

'He was like an animal.'

All the women of the town—and most especially Mrs. Taggart, the wife of a postman—John Joe had kept company with in his imagination. Mrs. Taggart was a well-built woman, a foot taller than himself, a woman with whom he had seen himself walking in the fields on the Ballydehob road. She had found him alone and had said that she was crossing the fields to where her husband had fallen into a bog-hole, and would he be able to come with her? She had a heavy, chunky face and a wide neck on which the fat lay in encircling folds, like a fleshy necklace. Her hair was grey and black, done up in hairpins. 'I was only codding you,' she said when they reached the side of a secluded hillock. 'You're a good-looking fellow, Dempsey.' On the side of the hillock, beneath a tree, Mrs. Taggart commenced to rid herself of her outer garments, remarking that it was hot. 'Slip out of that little jersey,' she urged. 'Wouldn't it bake you today?' Sitting beside him in her underclothes, Mrs. Taggart asked him if he liked sunbathing. She drew her petticoat up so that the sun might reach the tops of her legs. She asked him to put his hand on one of her legs so that he could feel the muscles; she was a strong woman, she said, and added that the strongest muscles she possessed were the muscles of her stomach. 'Wait till I show you,' said Mrs. Taggart.

On other occasions he found himself placed differently with Mrs. Taggart: once, his mother had sent him round to her house to inquire if she had any eggs for sale and after she had put a dozen eggs in a basket Mrs. Taggart asked him if he'd take a look at a thorn in the back of her leg. Another time he was passing her house and he heard her crying out for help. When he went inside he discovered that she had jammed the door of the bathroom and couldn't get out. He managed to release the door and when he entered the bathroom he discovered that Mrs. Taggart was standing up in the bath, seeming to have forgotten that she hadn't her clothes on.

Mrs. Keefe, the wife of a railway official, another statuesque woman, featured as regularly in John Joe's imagination, as did a Mrs. O'Brien, a Mrs. Summers, and a Mrs. Power. Mrs. Power kept a bread-shop, and a very pleasant way of passing the time when Brother Leahy was talking was to walk into Mrs. Power's shop and hear her saying that she'd have to slip into the bakery for a small pan loaf and would he like to accompany her? Mrs. Power wore a green overall with a belt that was tied in a knot at the front. In the bakery, while they were chatting, she would attempt to untie the belt but always found it difficult. 'Can you aid me?' Mrs. Power would ask and John

Joe would endeavour to loose the knot that lay tight against Mrs. Power's stout stomach. 'Where've you gone, boy?' Brother Leahy's voice would whisper over and over again like a familiar incantation and John Joe would suddenly shout, realizing he was in pain.

'It was the end of the war,' said Mr. Lynch. 'The following morning myself and a gang of the other lads got a train up to Liverpool, and then we crossed back to Dublin. There was a priest on the train and I spoke to him about the whole thing. Every man was made like that, he said to me, only I was lucky to be rescued in the nick of time. If I'd have taken his name I'd have sent him the information about my mother's dream. I think that would have interested him, John Joe. Wouldn't you think so?'

'Ah, it would of course.'

'Isn't it a great story, John Joe?'

'It is, Mr. Lynch.'

'Don't forget it ever, boy. No man is clear of temptations. You don't have to go to Britain to get temptations.'

'I understand you, Mr. Lynch.'

Quigley had said that one night he looked through a window and saw the Protestant clergyman, the Reverend Johnson, lying on the floor with his wife. There was another time, he said, that he observed Hickey the chemist being coaxed from an arm-chair by certain activities on the part of Mrs. Hickey. Quigley had climbed up on the roof of a shed and had seen Mrs. Swanton being helped out of her stockings by Swanton, the builder and decorator. Quigley's voice might continue for an hour and a half, for there was hardly a man and his wife in the town whom he didn't claim to have observed in intimate circumstances. John Joe did not ever ask how, when there was no convenient shed to climb on to, the dwarf managed to make his way to so many exposed upstairs windows. Such a question would have been wholly irrelevant.

At Mass, when John Joe saw the calves of women's legs stuck out from the kneeling position, he experienced an excitement that later bred new fantasies within him. 'That

Mrs. Dwyer,' he would say to the old dwarf, and the dwarf would reply that one night in February he had observed Mrs. Dwyer preparing herself for the return of her husband from a County Council meeting in Cork. From the powered body of Mrs. Dwyer, as described by Quigley, John Joe would move to an image that included himself. He saw himself pushing open the hall-door of the Dwyer's house, having been sent to the house with a message from his mother, and hearing Mrs. Dwyer's voice calling out, asking him to come upstairs. He stood on a landing and Mrs. Dwyer came to him with a red coat wrapped round her to cover herself up. He could smell the powder on her body; the coat kept slipping from her shoulders. 'I have some magazines for your mother,' she said. 'They're inside the bedroom.' He went and sat on the bed while she collected a pile of magazines. She sat beside him then, drawing his attention to a story here and there that might be of particular interest to his mother. Her knee was pressed against his, and in a moment she put her arm round his shoulders and said he was a good-looking lad. The red coat fell back on to the bed when Mrs. Dwyer took one of John Joe's large hands and placed it on her stomach. She then suggested, the evening being hot, that he should take off his jersey and his shirt.

Mrs. Keogh, the owner of the public house, had featured also in John Joe's imagination and in the conversation of the old dwarf. Quigley had seen her, he said, a week before her husband died, hitting her husband with a length of wire because he would not oblige her with his attentions. 'Come down to the cellar,' said Mrs. Keogh while Brother Leahy scribbled on the blackboard. 'Come down to the cellar, John Joe, and help me with a barrel.' He descended the cellar steps in front of her and when he looked back he saw her legs under her dark mourning skirt. 'I'm lost these days,' she said, 'since Mr. Keogh went on.' They moved the barrel together and then Mrs. Keogh said it was hot work and it would be better if they took off their jerseys. 'Haven't you the lovely arms!' she said as they rolled the barrel from one corner of the cellar to another. 'Will we lie down here for a rest?'

'We'll chance another bottle,' suggested Mr. Lynch. 'Is it going down you all right?'

'My mother'll be waiting for the rashers, Mr. Lynch.'

'No rasher can be cut, boy, till Mrs. Keogh returns. You could slice your hand off on an old machine like that.'

'We'll have one more so.'

At the Christian Brothers', jokes were passed about that concerned grisly developments in the beds of freshly wedded couples, or centred around heroes who carried by chance strings of sausages in their pockets and committed unfortunate errors when it came to cutting one off for the pan. Such yarns, succeeding generally, failed with John Joe, for they seemed to him to be lacking in quality.

'How's your mammy?' Mr. Lynch asked, watching John Joe pouring the stout.

'Ah, she's all right. I'm only worried she's waiting on the rashers——'

'There's honour due to a mother.'

John Joe nodded. He held the glass at an angle to receive dark foaming liquid, as Mr. Lynch had shown him. Mr. Lynch's mother, now seventy-nine, was still alive. They lived together in a house which Mr. Lynch left every morning in order to work in the office of a meal business and which he left every evening in order to drink bottles of stout in Keogh's. The bachelor state of Mr. Lynch was one which John Joe wondered if he himself would one day share. Certainly, he saw little attraction in the notion of marriage, apart from the immediate physical advantage. Yet Mr. Lynch's life did not seem enviable either. Often on Sunday afternoons he observed the meal clerk walking slowly with his mother on his arm, seeming as lost in gloom as the married men who walked beside women pushing prams. Quigley, a bachelor also, was a happier man than Mr. Lynch. He lived in what amounted to a shed at the bottom of his niece's garden. Food was carried to him, but there were few, with the exception of John Joe, who lingered in his company. On Sundays, a day which John Joe, like Mr. Lynch, spent with his mother, Quigley walked alone.

'When'll you be leaving the Brothers?' Mr. Lynch asked.

'In June.'

'And you'll be looking out for employment, John Joe?'

'I was thinking I'd go into the sawmills.'

Mr. Lynch nodded approvingly. 'There's a good future in the sawmills,' he said. 'Is the job fixed up?'

'Not yet, Mr. Lynch. They might give me a trial.'

Mr. Lynch nodded again, and for a moment the two sat in silence. John Joe could see from the thoughtful way Mr. Lynch was regarding his stout that there was something on his mind. Hoping to hear more about the Piccadilly tarts, John Joe patiently waited.

'If your daddy was alive,' said Mr. Lynch eventually, 'he might mention this to you, boy.'

He drank more stout and wiped the foam from his lips with the back of his hand. 'I often see you out with Quigley. Is it a good thing to be spending your hours with a performer like that? Quigley's away in the head.'

'You'd be sorry for the poor creature, Mr. Lynch.'

Mr. Lynch said there was no need to feel sorry for Quigley, since that was the way Quigley was made. He lit another cigarette. He said:

'Maybe they would say to themselves up at the sawmills that you were the same way as Quigley. If he keeps company with Quigley, they might say, aren't they two of a kind?'

'Ah, I don't think they'd bother themselves, Mr. Lynch. Sure, if you do the work well what would they have to complain of?'

'Has the manager up there seen you out with Quigley and the jam-jars?'

'I don't know, Mr. Lynch.'

'Everything I'm saying to you is for your own good in the future. Do you understand that? If I were in your shoes

I'd let Quigley look after himself.'

For years his mother had been saying the same to him. Brother Leahy had drawn him aside one day and had pointed out that an elderly dwarf wasn't a suitable companion for a young lad, especially since the dwarf was not sane. 'I see you took no notice of me,' Brother Leahy said six months later. 'Tell me this, young fellow-me-lad, what kind of a conversation do you have with old Quigley?' They talked, John Joe said, about trees and the flowers in the hedgerows. He liked to listen to Quigley, he said, because Quigley had acquired a knowledge of such matters. 'Don't tell me lies,' snapped Brother Leahy, and did not say anything else.

Mrs. Keogh returned from Confession. She came breathlessly into the bar, with pink cheeks, her ungloved hands the colour of meat. She was a woman of advanced middle age, a rotund woman who approached the proportions that John Joe most admired. She wore spectacles and had grey hair that was now a bit windswept. Her hat had blown off on the street, she said: she'd nearly gone mad trying to catch it. 'Glory be to God,' she cried when she saw John Joe. 'What's that fellow doing with a bottle of stout?'

'We had a man-to-man talk,' explained Mr. Lynch. 'I started him off on the pleasures of the bottle.'

'Are you mad? shouted Mrs. Keogh with a loud laugh. 'He's under age.'

' I came for rashers,' said John Joe. 'A pound of green rashers, Mrs. Keogh. The middle cut.'

'You're a shocking man,' said Mrs. Keogh to Mr. Lynch. She threw off her coat and hat. 'Will you pour me a bottle.' she asked, 'while I attend to this lad? Finish up that now, Mr. Dempsey.'

She laughed again. She went away and they heard from the grocery the sound of the bacon machine.

John Joe finished his stout and stood up.

'Good night, Mr. Lynch.'

'Remember about Quigley like a good fellow. When

the day will come that you'll want to find a girl to marry, she might be saying you were the same type as Quigley. D'you understand me, John Joe?'

'I do, Mr. Lynch.'

He passed through the door in the partition and watched Mrs. Keogh slicing the bacon. He imagined her, as Quigley had said he'd seen her, belabouring her late husband with a length of wire. He imagined her as he had seen her himself, taking off her jersey because it was hot in the cellar, and then unzipping her green tweed skirt.

'I've sliced it thin,' she said. 'It tastes better thin, I think."

'It does surely, Mrs. Keogh.'

'Are you better after your stout? Don't go telling your mammy now.' Mrs. Keogh laughed again, revealing long, crowded teeth. She weighed the bacon and wrapped it, munching a small piece of lean. 'If there's parsley in your mammy's garden,' she advised, chew a bit to get the smell of the stout away, in case she'd be cross with Mr. Lynch. Or a teaspoon of tea-leaves.'

'There's no parsley, Mrs. Keogh.'

'Wait till I get you the tea then.'

She opened a packet of tea and poured some on to the palm of his hand. She told him to chew it slowly and thoroughly and to let the leaves get into all the crevices of his mouth. She fastened the packet again, saying that no one would miss the little she'd taken from it. 'Four and two for the rashers,' she said.

He paid the money, with his mouth full of dry tea-leaves. He imagined Mrs. Keogh leaning on her elbows on the counter and asking him if he had a kiss for her at all, calling him Mr. Dempsey. He imagined her face stuck out towards his and her mouth open, displaying the big teeth, and her tongue damping her lips as the tongues of the Piccadilly tarts did, according to Mr. Lynch. With the dryness in his own mouth and a gathering uneasiness in his stomach, his lips would go out to hers and he would taste her saliva.

'Good night so, Mrs. Keogh.'

'Good night, Mr. Dempsey. Tell your mother I was asking for her.'

He left the public house. The wind which had dislodged Mrs. Keogh's hat felt fresh and cold on his face. The pink wash on a house across the street seemed pinker than it had seemed before, the ground moved beneath his feet, the street lighting seemed brighter. Youths and girls stood outside the illuminated windows of the small sweet-shops, waiting for the Coliseum to open. Four farmers left Regan's public house and mounted four bicycles and rode away, talking loudly. *Your Murphy Dealer* announced a large coloured sign in the window of a radio shop. Two boys that he had known at school came out of a shop eating biscuits from a paper bag. 'How're you, John Joe?' one of them said. 'How's Quigley these days?' They had left the school now: one of them worked in Kilmartin's the hardware's, the other in the Courthouse. They were wearing blue serge suits; their hair had been combed with care, and greased to remain tidy. They would go to the Coliseum, John Joe guessed, and sit behind two girls, giggling and whispering during the programme. Afterwards they would follow the girls for a little while, pretending to have no interest in them; they would buy chips in the chip-shop before they went home.

Thursday, Friday, Saturday, announced the sign outside the Coliseum: *The Rains Came.* As John Joe read them, the heavy black letters shifted, moving about on green paper that flapped in the wind, fixed with drawing-pins to an unpainted board. Mr. Daly, the owner of the grey Coliseum, arrived on his bicycle and unlocked his property. *Sunday Only: Spencer Tracy in Boom Town.* In spite of the sickness in his stomach and the unpleasant taste of tea-leaves in his mouth, John Joe felt happy and was aware of an inclination to loiter for a long time outside the cinema instead of returning to his mother.

'It's great tonight, John Joe,' Mr. Daly said. 'Are you coming in?'

John Joe shook his head. 'I have to bring rashers home to my mother,' he said. He saw Mrs. Daly approaching with a torch, for the small cinema was a family business. Every night and twice on Sundays, Mr. Daly sold the tickets while his wife showed the customers to their seats. 'I looked in a window one time,' Quigley had said, 'and she was trying to put on her undercloths. Daly was standing in his socks.'

A man and a girl came out of a sweet-shop next to the cinema, the girl with a box of Urney chocolates in her hand. She was thanking the man for them, saying they were lovely. 'It's a great show tonight, John Joe,' Mrs. Daly said, repeating the statement of her husband, repeating what she and he said every day of their lives. John Joe wagged his head at her. It looked a great show definitely, he said. He imagined her putting on her underclothes. He imagined her one night, unable because of a cold to show the customers to their seats, remaining at home in bed while her husband managed as best he could. 'I made a bit of bread for Mrs. Daly,' his mother said. 'Will you carry it down to her, John Joe?' He rang the bell and waited until she came to the door with a coat over her night-dress. He handed her the bread wrapped in creased brown paper and she asked him to step into the hall out of the wind. 'Will you take a bottle, John Joe?' Mrs. Daly said. He followed her into the kitchen, where she poured them each a glass of stout. 'Isn't it shocking hot in here?' she said. She took off her coat and sat at the kitchen table in her night-dress. 'You're a fine young fellow,' she said, touching his hand with her fingers.

John Joe walked on, past Riordan's the draper's and Kelly's Atlantic Hotel. A number of men were idling outside the entrance to the bar, smoking cigarettes, one of them leaning on a bicycle. 'There's a dance in Clonakilty,' a tall man said. 'Will we drive over to that?' The others took no notice of this suggestion. They were talking about the price of turkeys.

'How're you, John Joe?' shouted a red-haired youth

who worked in the sawmills. 'Quigley was looking for you.'

'I was up in Keogh's for my mother.'

'You're a decent man,' said the youth from the sawmills, going into the bar of Kelly's Hotel.

At the far end of North Street, near the small house where he lived with his mother, he saw Quigley, waiting for him. Once he had gone to the Coliseum with Quigley, telling his mother he was going with Kinsella, the boy who occupied the desk next to his at the Christian Brothers'. The occasion, the first and only time that Quigley had visited the Coliseum, had not been a success. Quigley hadn't understood what was happening and had become frightened. He'd begun to mutter and kick the seats in front of him. 'Take him off out of here,' Mr. Daly had whispered, flashing his wife's torch. 'He'll bring the house down.' They had left the cinema after only a few minutes and had gone instead to the chip-shop.

'I looked in a window last night,' said Quigley now, hurrying to his friend's side, 'and, God, I saw a great thing.'

'I was drinking stout with Mr. Lynch in Keogh's' said John Joe. He might tell Quigley about the glory girls that Mr. Lynch had advised him against, and about Baker who had struck a bargain with one of them, but it wouldn't be any use because Quigley never listened. No one held a conversation with Quigley: Quigley just talked.

'It was one o'clock in the morning,' said Quigley. His voice continued while John Joe opened the door of his mother's house and closed it behind him. Quigley would wait for him in the street and later on they'd perhaps go down to the chip-shop together.

'John Joe, where've you been?' demanded his mother, coming into the narrow hall from the kitchen. Her face was red from sitting too close to the range, her eyes had anger in them. 'What kept you, John Joe?'

'Mrs Keogh was at Confession.'

'What's that on your teeth?'

'What?'

'You've got dirt on your teeth.'

'I'll brush them then.'

He handed her the rashers. They went together to the kitchen, which was a small, low room with a flagged floor and a dresser that reached to the ceiling. On this, among plates and dishes, was the framed photograph of John Joe's father.

'Were you out with Quigley?' she asked, not believing that Mrs. Keogh had kept him waiting for more than an hour.

He shook his head, brushing his teeth at the sink. His back was to her, and he imagined her distrustfully regarding him, her dark eyes gleaming with a kind of jealousy, her small wiry body poised as if to spring on any lie he should utter. Often he felt when he spoke to her that for her the words came physically from his lips, that they were things she could examine after he'd ejected them, in order to assess their truth.

' I talked to Mr. Lynch,' he said. 'He was looking after the shop.'

'Is his mother well?'

'He didn't say.'

'He's very good to her.'

She unwrapped the bacon and dropped four rashers on to a pan that was warming on the range. John Joe sat down at the kitchen table. The feeling of euphoria that had possessed him outside the Coliseum was with him no longer; the floor was steady beneath his chair.

'They're good rashers,' his mother said.

'Mrs. Keogh cut them thin.'

'They're best thin. They have a nicer taste.'

'Mrs. Keogh said that.'

'What did Mr. Lynch say to you? Didn't he mention the old mother?'

'He was talking about the war he was in.'

'It nearly broke her heart when he went to join it.'

'It was funny all right.'

'We were a neutral country.'

Mr. Lynch would be still sitting in the bar of Keogh's. Every night of his life he sat there with his hat on his head, drinking bottles of stout. Other men would come into the bar and he would discuss matters with them and with Mrs. Keogh. He would be drunk at the end of the evening. John Joe wondered if he chewed tea so that the smell of stout would not be detected by his mother when he returned to her. He would return and tell her some lies about where he had been. He had joined the British Army in order to get away from her for a time, only she'd reached out to him from a dream.

'Lay the table, John Joe.'

He put a knife and a fork for each of them on the table, and found butter and salt and pepper. His mother cut four pieces of griddle bread and placed them to fry on the pan. 'I looked in a window one time,' said the voice of Quigley, 'and Mrs. Sullivan was caressing Sullivan's legs.'

'We're hours late with the tea,' his mother said. 'Are you starving, pet?'

'Ah, I am, definitely.'

'I have nice fresh eggs for you.'

It was difficult for her sometimes to make ends meet. He knew it was, yet neither of them had ever said anything. When he went to work in the sawmills it would naturally be easier, with a sum each week to add to the pension.

She fried the eggs, two for him and one for herself. He watched her basting them in her expert way, intent upon what she was going. Her anger was gone, now that he was safely in the kitchen, waiting for the food she cooked. Mr. Lynch would have had his tea earlier in the evening, before he went down to Keogh's. 'I'm going out for a long walk,' he probably said to his mother, every evening after he'd wiped the egg from around his mouth.

'Did he tell you an experience he had in the war?' his mother asked, placing the plate of rashers, eggs and fried bread in front of him. She poured boiling water into a brown enamel tea-pot and left it on the range to draw.

'He told me about a time they were attacked by the Germans,' John Joe said. 'Mr. Lynch was nearly killed.'

'She thought he'd never come back.'

'Oh, he came back all right.'

'He's very good to her now.'

When Brother Leahy twisted the short hairs on his neck and asked him what he'd been dreaming about he usually said he'd been working something out in his mind, like a long division sum. Once he said he'd been trying to translate a sentence into Irish, and another time he'd said he'd been solving a puzzle that had appeared in the *Sunday Independent.* Recalling Brother Leahy's face, he ate the fried food. His mother repeated that the eggs were fresh. She poured him a cup of tea.

'Have you homework to do?'

He shook his head, silently registering that lie, knowing that there was homework to be done, but wishing instead to accompany Quigley to the chip-shop.

'Then we can listen to the wireless,' she said.

'I thought maybe I'd go out for a walk.'

Again the anger appeared in her eyes. Her mouth tightened, she laid down her knife and fork.

'I thought you'd stop in, John Joe,' she said, 'on your birthday.'

'Ah, well now——'

'I have a little surprise for you.'

She was telling him lies, he thought, just as he had told her lies. She began to eat again, and he could see in her face a reflection of the busyness that had developed in her mind. What could she find to produce as a surprise? She had given him that morning a green shirt that she knew he'd like because he liked the colour. There was a cake that she'd made, some of which they'd have when they'd eaten what was in front of them now. He knew about this birthday cake because he had watched her decorating it with hundreds and thousands: she couldn't suddenly say it was a surprise.

'When I've washed the dishes,' she said, 'we'll listen to

out.' From the wireless came the voice of a man advertising household products. 'Bird's Custard,' urged the voice gently, 'and Bird's Jelly De Luxe.'

He filled the pen from the bottle of ink she handed him. He sat down at the kitchen table and tried the nib out on the piece of brown paper that Mrs. Keogh had wrapped round the rashers and which his mother had neatly folded away for further use.

'Isn't it great it works still?' she said. 'It must be a good pen.'

It's hot in here, he wrote. *Wouldn't you take off your jersey?* 'That's a funny thing to write,' his mother said.

'It came into my head.'

They didn't like him being with Quigley because they knew what Quigley talked about when he spoke the truth. They were jealous because there was no pretence between Quigley and himself. Even though it was only Quigley who talked, there was an understanding between them: being with Quigley was like being alone.

'I want you to promise me a thing.' she said, 'now that you're fifteen.'

He put the cap on the pen and bundled up the paper that had contained the rashers. He opened the top of the range and dropped the paper into it. She would ask him to promise not to hang about with the town's idiot any more. He was a big boy now, he was big enough to own his father's fountain-pen and it wasn't right that he should be going out getting minnows in a jam-jar with an elderly affected creature. It wouud go against his chances in the saw-mills.

He listened to her saying what he had anticipated she would say. She went on talking, telling him about his father and the goodness there had been in his father before he fell from the scaffold. She took from the dresser the framed photograph that was so familiar to him and she put it into his hands, telling him to look closely at it. It would have made no difference, he thought, if his father had lived. His father would have been like the others; if ever he'd have dared to mention the nakedness of Mrs. Taggart his father would have beaten him with a belt.

'I am asking you for his sake,' she said, 'as much as for my own and for yours, John Joe.'

He didn't understand what she meant by that, and he didn't inquire. He would say what she wished to hear him say, and he would keep his promise to her because it would be the easiest thing to do. Quigley wasn't hard to push away, you could tell him to get away like you'd tell a dog. It was funny that they should think that it would make much difference to him now, as this stage, not having Quigley to listen to.

'All right,' he said.

'You're a good boy, John Joe. Do you like the pen?'

'It's a lovely pen.'

'You might write better with that one.'

She turned up the volume of the wireless and together they sat by the range, listening to the music. To live in a shed like Quigley did would not be too bad: to have his food carried down through a garden by a niece, to go about the town in that special way, alone with his thoughts. Quigley did not have to pretend to the niece who fed him. He didn't have to say he'd been for a walk when he'd been drinking in Keogh's or that he'd been playing cards with men when he'd been dancing in Clonakilty; Quigley didn't have to chew tea and keep quiet. Quigley talked; he said the words he wanted to say. Quigley was lucky being how he was.

'I will go to bed now,' he said eventually.

They said good night to one another, and he climbed the stairs to his room. She would rouse him in good time, she called after him. 'Have a good sleep,' she said.

He closed the door of his room and looked with affection at his bed, for in the end there was only that. It was a bed that, sagging, held him in its centre and wrapped him warmly. There was ornamental brass-work at the head but not at the foot, and on the web of interlocking wire the hair mattress was thin. John Joe shed his clothes, shedding also the small town and his mother and Mr. Lynch and the fact that he, on his fifteenth birthday, had drunk his first stout and had chewed tea. He entered his iron bed and the face of Mr. Lynch passed from his mind and the voices of boys telling stories about freshly married couples faded away also. No one said to him now that he must not keep company with a crazed dwarf. In his iron bed, staring into the darkness, he made of the town what he wished to make of it, knowing that he would not be drawn away from his dreams by the tormenting fingers of a Christian Brother. In his iron bed he heard again only the voice of the town's idiot and then that voice, too, was there no more. He travelled alone, visiting in his way the women of the town, adored and adoring, more alive in his bed than ever he was at the Christian Brothers' School, or in the grey Coliseum, or in the chip-shop, or Keogh's public house, or his mother's kitchen, more alive than ever he would be at the sawmills. In his bed he entered a paradise: it was grand being alone.

KEVIN CASEY

Priest and People

The priest was a tall man, gaunt as a rake, with stooped shoulders and receding grey hair. His fingers were long and very pointed, constantly moving as if he were a pianist practising some elaborate scale. Kneeling on the steps of the altar, his back to the people, he looked about forty but when he stood and turned, his face, faded to parchment by the suns of India, was old and uncompromising. His black soutane was well worn and a little too short; the trousers edge that showed beneath it, frayed; the shoes highly polished but badly cracked. He cleared his throat, his long fingers covering the action, then moving across his nose and resting on his cheek as he looked down at the thread-bare red carpet.

The peopie stirred with apprehension. It was the third night of the mission and already the missioner had a reputation in the parish. He had preached the first sermon; the young priest had preached to them on the second night, a quiet sermon, well larded with reliable anecdotes and everyone thought he was very nice, but this man's talk was straight from the shoulder. No stories, no jokes, only occasional consolatory glimmers of hope. 'I'm here to talk facts,' he said, and the facts had led to lengthy queues out-side the confession box on the following morning.

The priest cleared his throat again and, hooking his thumbs into the cloth girdle he wore around his waist, looked down the church. The men were all on the gospel side of the nave, the women on the epistle. There wasn't a single place left vacant. He saw the faces of the people as a blur, colours were in patches, the teacher, kneeling in the tiny gallery beside the harmonium, was a black shape against the darkening colours of the stained glass window. He had trouble with his eyes, but was strangely unwilling to admit to even the slightest physical defect.

My dear brethren, he said, his voice loud and resonant, trained to battle with the acoustics of cathedral and church, *I am pleased to see such a good attendance at the mission to-night. I am pleased and I know that Almighty God is pleased. He is generous, more generous than any earthly friend can ever be and He is constantly offering to us all His divine grace. But it is at a time such as this, the time of a mission, when we lay aside the work of the day and engage, by prayer and instruction and examination of conscience, in a spiritual stocktaking, that His generosity has no limits. He will pour His graces on this church to-night as He poured manna on the desert long ago. He will speak to each and everyone of you, perhaps through my poor voice, perhaps through some inner stirring in your heart. If you will give your heart and soul to Him, He will enter and work wonders. He is seeking you then, asking for admittance. The time of a mission is the time for the breaking of all the locks and bolts that you set around yourself through love of the world and the flesh. Break them! Now is your chance. You may never have another. Remember that, dear brethren. You may be within minutes of your time now. Don't allow yourself be caught with a hardened heart when the sweat of death is breaking out on your brow. For if you ignore His generosity and refuse His love; if you do these things by not attending your mission or attending it in body only but not in spirit, then you spit on His face, you scourge His body, you hammer the crown of thorns onto His sacred head. And can you then depend on His mercy when you have refused His love? No! you earn then the terrible wrath of a just God.*

The muffled coughs, the feet scraping on the bare boards, the beads held tightly in sweating hands, the old faces alert with agreement, the young faces with no real comprehension, the indifferent faces, the lethargic faces, the faces screwed tightly with determined concentration; all these he missed. The people were indistinct rows, made in the image and likeness of God; he was the instrument who would gather them into the barn of their maker.

To-night, he said, *it is my intention to speak on a most important subject. Listen carefully and it may be the cause of your salvation from a most serious sin. Modesty and chastity are two virtues most pleasing in the eyes of God and His Blessed Mother. These virtues. . . .*

The teacher was sixty-three. Twenty-one years in charge of the village school had made him old and wise and full of worldly understanding. Kneeling in the small gallery, the heads of the people beneath him, the voice of the missioner loud in his ears, he noticed, without emotion, the thin rustle of excitement that passed amongst the girls when the subject of the sermon was announced. Modesty and chastity, he thought, the ever reliable subjects for altar step oratory. If the people were modest and the people were chaste, half the priests in the country would be out of business. He smiled as he drew a mental picture of a winding queue of black-coated figures, big and small, outside a labour exchange, then with a small cough, as if guilty of being caught in some sin, wiped it from his mind as he would a chalk drawing from the blackboard and thought of the subject again. Modesty and chastity, elusive virtues.

. . . to all the women out of respect for His own mother,' said the priest. *'That is why it is so disturbing to hear that in this very parish there is a girl who openly flaunts herself in sin. The devil owns this girl, body and soul and you, the people, must feel ashamed. . . .*

She clenched her fingers together and lowered her eyes. The beat of her heart frightened her. It seemed to have lost all regularity. She moved her right foot up and down on the floor. The small, brown, pointed shoe made a tapping noise. The voice of the missioner seemed stentorian now. The blood was warm against her cheeks. She longed to unbutton her coat. She knew that she shouldn't have come; she hadn't wanted to come, it was only to satisfy her mother. All right, she thought, let him say what he likes.

He doesn't know what he's talking about anyway. Let him paint every colour with the dirty black of mortal sin. I don't care.

. . . *a source of scandal,* said the priest. *Brazenly defiant. Trying to forget about the punishment that is just reward of sin. I have seen girls like that before. I have seen loose women who thought nothing of sinning with any man. But mark my words. Their sin is, in the eyes of God, hideous and. . . .*

He shouldn't have been told about it, thought the teacher. To give our priest his due, I don't think he would have told him if he thought she would be here. She was coming to nothing but Mass on Sunday and I know he feared scandal. But even so, he shouldn't have been told. These men in their monasteries grow inwards and the tragic thing about it is that they take this to be the growth towards God. But it's always God in relation to themselves; a judgment of themselves and others on their own standards. Shifting standards. Nobody on earth is so liable to fall into the way of the Pharisee as the priest; they can't put themselves into the position of others and examine a problem from that angle. Their own vow of chastity distorts their vision of the feelings of ordinary humanity. I often feel that it's this kind of spiritual selfishness that ruins the relationship of a priest with his people. He's speaking now as a priest, wise perhaps, but frighteningly ignorant of the mind of a girl of twenty.

. . . *occasion of sin,* said the priest. *Hear this now and be ever attentive to it. It is a sin for a boy and girl to be together in a lonely place. For it is lonely places. . . .*

I don't regret it, she thought. That's old woman's talk. He never knew the sensations I have known. It was a lonely place all right. But God, it was beautiful. It was really beautiful. The river was smooth and silver and the reflection of the moon in it was hardly broken at all. The trees and the grass were very green. I remember I said to him. Did you ever before see grass as green as this? He laughed, and said, Of course I did! Go away out of that, I said, I was told that everything in England was black as soot.

If I had any courage, thought the teacher, even one, single shred of it, I'd stand up now and I'd say, Listen, Father, you might mean well but you're talking through your biretta. It is not a sin for a girl and boy to be together in a lonely place. It's a natural thing, that's what it is, it is an understandable thing. Then I'd sit down with a a job well done. But like generations who have gone before me I lack courage at a time like this and I try to content myself with mental derision. I wonder what a lonely place is. I couldn't give a definition very easily and I don't think that he could either. A place is as lonely as you make it. I have been lonely in the city. I have been lonely at parties; amongst all the merriment I felt deserted. That party, then, was a lonely place for me. Would the presence of a girl have been a sin? There were no difference between it and the bucolic versions that these men from their monasteries love to quote. The interesting thing is that I have been miles from anyone or any place, in the country, without any loneliness. They forget that the love of a boy for a girl is an imitation of the great love, the love of man for God. Just take away the physical, and the same need, the same longing exists. So that just as they go away from others so that nothing may come between themselves and God, a boy and girl will also avoid others, so that nothing can spoil the tenderness of the feeling that exists between them. If it is ever to come to blossom, love needs that kind of loneliness. God knows I can't claim to be an authority on moral theology but I'm certain that I'm correct.

. . . with only one thing in mind, said the priest, *their own sinful pleasure.*

Her mother was rigid as a stone. She hadn't expected anything like this. There was always a sermon on company-keeping but never before had she heard such a denouncement, And everybody must know that he was talking about her daughter. She felt sorry now that she had forced her to come, but she had done so for her own good. She thought that some grace might be given or some words said that would cause, or even help her towards contrition. It was terrible for a girl to have a serious sin on her soul and to refuse to confess it; to claim that she could never feel sorrow. Only a year ago she was a tall girl, gay, with no secrets; now she was a woman with a whole treasure house of new knowledge that was shielded in her heart. It was frightening when your children grew away from you like that. Suddenly, you felt old and useless and a portion of your life was whisked away.

. . . kiss a girl until they are engaged to be married. Even then strict modesty must be observed. The kiss is a token of love, not a symbol of lust.

They had sat together near the edge of the wood, where the river passed slowly towards the bridge and the village. Meath was rich around her. With him her body had a whole new life; pain and pleasure surging through her. He had kissed her and kissed her until she felt that all the strength in her body had been drawn away by his strength. Close against him, his lips on her neck, on her cheek, on her mouth, she had clung to him and cried softly and consented to his whispered question knowing that to refuse now would be to live forever with gnawing thoughts of deep regret.

. . . woe unto him. God is not mocked. And woe unto her. I tell you this and I say it to you before God Who is my judge just as He is hers. Unless she repents of sins of the flesh she will burn forever in the agonising flames of hell.

Her father wondered who he was talking about. He had heard of no trouble in the parish. Shotgun weddings weren't uncommon and you'd hear now and then of some girl leaving for England in a hurry, but this seemed different. There had never been such a fuss before; it must be serious. He wondered again who it could be and glanced over at the women and the girls. He would ask someone as soon as he left the church.

The people looked at the priest. They heard his words with a variety of emotion. Those in front of her found it difficult to resist the temptation of turning to have a look; those behind her looked at her back, then at the face of the priest and at her back again, waiting for some sign from the body beneath the white scarf and old, blue coat. Most of the girls felt sorry for her and a little uneasy for themselves. The line between one person and another is very thin, a mere thread of accidental circumstances. It could be ignorance or innocence or contingence or a father's belt. And a deep rooted, instinctive fear, the fear of the hunted, the fear of being caught.

. . . most girls are pure, thank God, said the priest, *because they come from good Catholic homes. But the best apples may have a rotten fruit amongst them and it is this fruit that will contaminate others.*

He's going too far, thought the teacher. Can a man no longer stand in sacerdotal shoes and knows when words are verbal excess? Can fast and flagellation destroy all feelings? Priest or no priest, he's not God Almighty. Does he really think that he's helping anyone by talking like that when the girl and her mother are here; by throwing charity to the winds when it comes to chastity?

Most girls are pure!, she thought, and she had to smile although the muscles in her face seemed to be pulled tight. There isn't one of them, not a single one who wouldn't have had him if they got the chance. I know that. I saw the way they were looking at him. They're probably pleased now, but there was never yet a girl with smugness on her face who hadn't got envy somewhere in her heart. Maybe they feel sorry for me; I don't want their sorrow. Let them offer it to me and I'll throw it back into their faces. I don't feel sorrow; I will never feel sorrow. Contrition would be a betrayal of a moment that was beautiful, a betrayal of myself. There was nothing ugly about it and you need some ugliness for sin. Maybe it was a little the first time, but that's because it was new and new things always frighten me. But afterwards . . . sorrow would be a mockery.

. . . *must spend the rest of their lives regretting it*, said the priest, *for they lose the most precious possession a young girl can have and no decent self-respecting man will have anything to do with them. They throw it away to someone who has no respect for them, who just wants to use them, and when he has spent his lust he casts them aside as you would an old shoe.*

That isn't the way it was at all, she thought. He didn't throw me aside. That was just the way things were. Maybe he should have told me that he was married, at the start, but I'm not sorry that he didn't. It wouldn't have made any difference. It hurt when he told me, it shattered so many dreams, but I had reality to remember and that's better than looking forward to dreams. He wasn't happy with his wife; he told me that, but there was a child whom they both loved and that was their only bond. He never knew about ours, he warned me to be careful; he used ask me every evening but I didn't care. He left because he had to leave. It isn't true to say that he threw me aside.

. . . *their mothers. Their unfortunate mothers. Maybe they aren't to blame. It is possible that they have done their best. But still their best was not enough and they have a lot an answer for. . . .'*

I always did my best for her, thought her mother. God knows I did. She felt ashamed of the tears in her eyes and was terribly conscious of the women around her. Maybe I loved her too much; a mother can make that mistake. I spent most of my time protecting her from her father. I hated to see him raise his hand to her; it isn't right for a man to strike a girl. But that might have been a mistake. A few good beatings then might have prevented all this. I remember when she first told me about it, she hadn't been looking well and I had gone to her room to ask her if there was anything I could do. And she told me then. I said no cross word to her. The first thing I said was 'Your father mustn't hear about this.' It was foolish, of course. He had to know some time and its only worse now. It should have been so serious but it became a kind of joke between us; the morning he said to me, 'That one is getting very stout. She's sitting around the house too much.' And the way the two of us laughed afterwards when I told her about it. But I did want her to go to Confession and Communion; I asked her to pray for contrition if she couldn't find it in her heart but she only shook her head. Then I heard about the mission and I made sure that she'd attend. I thought that something might be said that would change things.

. . . sold herself for even less than the thirty pieces of silver, said the priest. *She had sold herself body and soul for a sinful carnal pleasure and truly earned the wrath of God.*

Her father, his two hands on his knees, the unaccustomed collar tight around his neck, sat motionless. He hoped that this would be a lesson to his daughter. He didn't like all that dancing and staying out late at night. But she had quietened down a lot recently. Maybe she had heard about it and learned from it. A girl should learn from a thing like that. It was good for them to find out what men nowadays were looking for. He felt sorry for the father of the girl the priest was talking about. That man would find it difficult to face his neighbours. His curiosity got the better of him. He nudged the man who was sitting beside him and whispered, 'Who is she?'

The man was small and sallow with long strands of hair plastered across his head in a futile attempt to hide baldness.

'What's that?' he asked nervously, his voice a faint whisper from behind closed teeth.

'What girl is he talking about? Who's in trouble?'

The man looked at him nervously. His little restless eyes took in every detail of his face.

'I don't know man,' he said, 'I'm not sure.'

The virtue of purity, said the priest, *is the most pleasing of virtues in the eyes of the Mother of God who was herself most pure. In his Confessions, the great Saint Augustine gives us an idea of the depths of degradation to which the impure may sink. My one desire, he writes, was to love and to be loved. But in this I did not keep the measure of mind to mind which is the luminous line of friendship, but from the muddy concupisence of the flesh and the hot imagination of puberty, mists steamed up to becloud and darken my heart so that I could not distinguish the white light of love from the fog of lust. Both love and lust boiled within me and swept my youthful immaturity over the precipice of evil desires to leave me half drowned in a whirlpool of abominable sins. Your wrath had grown mighty against me and I knew it not.*

'You don't know?'

'I'm not sure man.'

Her father looked carefully at the man beside him. He seemed very nervous. He wondered why his question had met with this reaction.

. . . the intoxication of the invisible wine of will perverted and turned towards baseness.

He looked straight ahead of him and looked at the priest. But he didn't hear the words. It isn't, he said to himself, no that's foolish, I'd know about it long ago, not at all it isn't, but still I noticed that lately she's sitting around the house a lot and . . . ah not at all, it couldn't be.

. . . walked the streets of Babylon, said the priest, *and wallowed in its filth as if it had been a bed of spices and precious ornaments.*

Oh Augustine, Augustine, thought the teacher, can the words of a man wise at forty-five be justly quoted against a girl foolish at twenty? Did you write them in praise, Augustine, of a God Who had showed you mercy or in anger against a God Who had allowed you sink so low? So low, remember, that when you rose you were the bigger and the greater for it. There was mercy for you, Augustine, why shouldn't there me mercy for everyone else in God's own good time?

He had whispered his question.
'Yes,' she said.
'In love?'
'Yes, Love.'
'I was in love,' she thought, 'in love, in love, in love. . . .'

'To abuse love,' said the priest, *'to offer insult instead of praise.'*

'If they really loved you God,' thought the teacher, 'they would love you for Your mercy and fear You for Your wrath. Without Your mercy, what one of us can pass through the eye of an needle?'

Saint Paul has written that no fornicator or unclean soul hath inheritance in the Kingdom of Heaven. Run through all the sins, said Saint Isidore, you will find none to equal this crime.

It surely couldn't be, thought her father. She was never that kind. Wild maybe and a bit carefree, but not that kind.

The hand of God will descend in wrath, said the priest, *and they will wither like leaves before it.*

Magdalen, thought the teacher, Magdalen, greatest of all the Saints. You showed her her folly in Your own good time. Who are we to talk as if we had Your eyes?

She closed her eyes tightly.
Oh Almighty God, she prayed, please listen to me. I don't ask You for forgiveness if I have offended You. Maybe some day it will be different. But I love You God. All I ask for now is understanding and I know that You will give me that."
She left her seat, genuflected and walked down the aisle. She felt the anticipation and excitment of the people; she saw the white face of her mother and the red, sweating face of her father.

The priest was nearing the end of his sermon. There was

a dull pain at the back of his eyes. He shut them and pressed tightly on the lids with the tips of his fingers. The pain could sometimes be relieved that way. He sensed the new atmosphere surrounding the people and knew that he was holding them no longer. He offered up his pain.

TOM MAC INTYRE

An Aspect of the Rising

Opposite Adam and Eve's, the up-river east wind that would frizzle a mermaid's fins a zephyr tickle the second I sighted her. Plump chiaroscuro: black bobbed hair, white cheeks, black coat, white calves, black shoes, high-heeling along the far footpath. She looked recklessly like herself, in her wisdom gazed neither to the left nor to the right but let the plastic bag winking on her rump com'ither me through the scooting traffic and urgent to her side.

'We're in business' — I matched her step, leaned towards her, eager as a guitar.

'Fast from the trap, aren't you' — she spoke from the lips out, never slackened pace — 'wonder you weren't made ointment of crossing the street.'

'You're beautiful' — pursuing, I ladled compliments into her small skintight ear, and now she coy'd. The black pencilled line above her visible eye, the right, took my admiration. Oblique but eloquent of the horizontal, a masterpiece. still we hurried——

'Where're we going?'

'You have a car?'

Had a car.

'I have to have a cup of coffee' — her mauve mouth belonged to the first woman, the destined rib — 'You can get the car. And wait for me up here outside The Last Post.'

She went. Captive, I watched her buttocks acclaim a royal leaving. Her scent stayed. A firm scent. And ready. Appled. That was it. Apples and muscles. Taffeta flashing above her bright-bare calves, the door of The Last Post opened before her.

Philomena, she introduced herself. And my instinct, I decided, had been sound. Anything with ears on it bar a pot is the rule along the river most nights but here was a real professional, her every motion *credo*——

'How're they hanging?' she enquired as we drove off towards Kingsbridge and The Park beyond.

'Two eggs in a hanky.'

Chuckling, she produced cigarettes, lit two, and passed one to me. They were Polish and smuggled—a sailor from Riga.

'Poles, I say to him,' she reminisced, settling back in the seat — knees sudden and vocal as the skirt rose, 'poles is right.'

Sure of your wares is sure of your stares. Philomena, slowly, fingered open her coat, and — I glanced across — the wares, big unbiddable breasts, trim belly, and roomy thighs, began to move and converse under blouse and skirt as if equally sure of themselves. To the silencer in these excitements I bowed. She reading me with black eyes, understood, and, leaning over, petted my abundant crotch. Jesus, I thought — giddy — I'll have to be dug out of her. The last buses were being shunted home, on the roof of The Brewery a bouncy moon. Apples and the contraband of The Baltic odorous about us, we took the hill, sped through the gates and into The Park.

'Here, Philomena?'

A few hundred yards in, and impetuous, I was steering for a convenient nest under the adjacent and glooming trees.

'No, keep going. Right. Keep going. There's a little spot I know. I'll show you the way'——

Venue. Between friends, I asked, what was the difference, here or there? No good. We drove. Insistent, she directed me, her neat coaxing hand slipping in and out of the light—'It's a special spot I have. Not far——'

On reflection, I yielded. She was right. Not any hole in

the wall but a sanctified lair. What a woman! We passed The Zoo. A lion raged within, and down to our right flamingoes fluttered and gossiped in the pink insomnia of their watery bed.

'The Zoo's grand,' she voiced dreamily. 'Keep going.'

Open spaces, right, left, this fork now, trees, silver choppy in the branches, no trees, silver seamless along the grass. Delay's a randy foreman. I glimpsed the dank remains of turfstacks which had warmed Dublin winters ago, I glimpsed the long-legged ghosts of slaughtered deer but I thought neither of the huddled fire nor the red jittery stag. She sat there, relaxed, substantial in the run of shadows, now and then nibbling my neck.

'Nearly there.'

'Christ,' I grouched, 'we'll be at The Boyne before we know it.'

Next moment—'Here,' she pointed, 'left——'

And (it wasn't just the voice, curiously level) I felt—alteration. On the turn, I inspected her. Sure enough, she was tight in the seat, tight as Christy's britches. Suspicion cranked me. No, I calmed myself. The cramp of an instant. It means nothing. We were driving towards a stand of fir and pine a hundred yards away, a large building visible in fragmented outline beyond. Deep into the trees, I pulled up. Philomena, my new Philomena, was out of the car, wordless, before I'd switched off the ignition. Worried, I followed.

Smell of the trees. And the place's seasoned privacy. And the midnight dusk. There she was — a stranger and grim — her back to a young fir a few yards off. What was she at? Climbing the palisade of her remove, I advanced. Rhinestones flickered but didn't beckon. I was beside her, whispering. Weep for my whispers. She was wood against that tree. My fingers implored. Colder than wood——

'What's wrong?'

Two bleak eyes, she stood there. I made a rude remark. It passed lightly through her — your hand through a ghost.

'What is it?' I tried again, 'What's wrong?'

Useless, I scanned her face, a hunter's face, stalking what? Wind skidded on the branches. Philomena and I waited. For five stinging seconds, and then the spurs of a mean anger raked me. Let me omit the vituperation I flung upon her. It shames my balls, and it balls my shame. Tranced black and white in a shaft of the moon, she paid, thank God, no heed. I wheeled to depart, and not three steps had I taken when the woman, catspitting, was soaring to her singular and sainted glory——

'You crawthumpin' get of a Spaniard that never was seen' — incredulous, I stopped: the wood rang — 'with your long features and your long memory and your two and twenty-two strings to your bow, what crooked eggs without yolks are you hatching between Rosaries tonight?'

Birds racketing. The Spaniard? To a skelp of joy, I connected. The building beyond — Arus an Uachtarain, de Valera himself under sharp and sharpening fire——

'Diagrams', I heard, 'diagrams' — and a sneer bisected the word as it flew — 'more of them you're amusing yourself with maybe, proving that A is B and B is C and a Republic is Jazus knows what until Euclid himself'd be cracked in Dundrum trying to make y'out. But Professor Isosceles' — she drew harsh breath, raced on, discovering the beat of her scorn — 'it was damn all diagrams or anything else we got from you above in Boland's Mills when Simon Donnelly had to take over the command, you sitting there with your heart in your gob and your arse in a sling——'

Listen to me. There are sights you never forget. Her face wild, throat wilder, hands two kicking lanterns, knees ivory below — immobile and smooth, Philomena roasted The Long Fellow. Practice graced her, rancours unnameable and a fury of the bones powered her — she left nothing out, there was nothing she didn't fit in: The Treaty, The Civil War, The Oath, The Hangings of the 40s, Emigration, Inflation, Taxation, The Language, the lot. An eighth of a mile away, brooding or at his prayers,

His excellency heard not a word but, chosen by The Gods, I heard, the ground heard and the wind and the sky's cupped ear. We listened to that alto scurrility leap the air, listened in ecstasy and heard — reaches distant — backlane and gutter answer, stir, shift, and jig maddened to an old, a blithe, a bitter tune——

'You,' she cried aloud and aloft, 'you long spear in the side of a Christian people, May God drop a clog on you, May the Divil make a knot of you, May coals scorch you and may cinders choke you, May smoke annoy you and may soot destroy you, May the day peel your skins and the night screech your sins, May . . . .'

Don't ask me how long it lasted but bring back Moses and I'll say it to his teeth: she finished that diatribe a creature of flame. You'd kneel to her——

'You there,' says she—there was barely a pause—into the shriven quiet, 'Are you comin' or goin'?'

I was dazzled but comin'. Gaily she murmured me in. Zips purred. The undergrowth lured. To it we went, and at it we stayed.

Birds settled again on the branches. In the great house beyond the trees — lights burning here and there, in the city below, and all over Ireland, medals were being dusted, ribbons spruced, orations polished and artillery oiled for The Fiftieth Anniversary of The Insurrection.